THE KING NOBODY WANTED

The King nobody wanted

By NORMAN F. LANGFORD

Illustrated by John Lear

THE WESTMINSTER PRESS

PHILADELPHIA

Printed in the United States of America
At The Lakeside Press
R. R. Donnelley & Sons Company, Chicago
and Crawfordsville, Indiana

CONTENTS

ABOUT THIS BOOK

In a very real and interesting way, THE KING NOBODY WANTED *tells the story of Jesus. Where the actual words of the Bible are used, they are from the King James Version. But the greater part of the story is told in the words of every day.*

Since you will certainly want to look up these stories in your own Bible, the references are given on pages 191 and 192. You will discover that often more than one Gospel tells the same story about Jesus, but in a slightly different way. In THE KING NOBODY WANTED, *the stories from the Gospels have been put together so that there is just one story for you to read and understand and enjoy.*

1. Waiting

Two THOUSAND years ago, in the land of Palestine, the Jewish people were waiting for something to happen—or, really, were waiting for someone to come.

"When will he come?" was the question they were always asking one another. "Will he come in five years? next year? Or is he already on his way?"

They were waiting for someone, and when he came they would call him "the Messiah." If they spoke the Greek language, they would call him "Christ." The people thought he would be a great king.

7

They had one king already. His name was Herod the Great. But Herod was not the kind of king they wanted. Herod was hard and cruel. He poisoned and beheaded those who made him angry. He was not a Jew by birth. The Messiah, when *he* came, would be a good king. He would be a Jew himself, and a friend to all the Jewish people. One of the prophets said he would be like the shepherds of Palestine, who watched their sheep night and day, and carried the small lambs in their arms.

But the most important thing about the Messiah was that he would drive Caesar and his armies out of the country. Caesar! How they hated his very name! For Caesar was the emperor of the Romans. Some years before, the Romans had occupied the country and begun to rule it. Herod was still king of the Jews, but now he took his orders from Caesar. Everybody had to take orders from Caesar. The Jews were not a free people any more.

"It used to be so different," the older people sighed, "before the Romans came."

Everywhere in Palestine Roman armies went marching. Their shields flashed in the sunlight, and when they were on the march they carried golden eagles which stood for Caesar's power.

The Romans tried to rule the country well. They said that everybody would get justice and fair play. But the Jews could not see the fairness in having to pay taxes to a foreign king who did not even worship

God. They did not like to see Roman soldiers whipping people with long leather whips called scourges, into which bits of glass and lead and iron were fastened to make them bite more deeply into some poor Jew's back. They were sick at heart when the Romans began to punish criminals by nailing them up by their hands and feet to big wooden crosses, and leaving them to hang there until they died.

Well, the Messiah would take care of the Romans. He would gather an army from east and west and north and south. Then there would be a great day for the Jewish people, a great day for the nation that was called by the glorious name of Israel! From all over the country the men of Israel would rise up. They would come when their king called them, and he would lead them to victory against Caesar. The Romans would go back where they came from, and Israel would be free and peaceful and rich and happy again. The Messiah would make Israel into a great kingdom, bigger and more powerful than the Roman Empire ever was. The Jews would rule the world. Everyone, everywhere, would worship the God of Israel, and the Messiah would be King of all the nations of the earth. If only he would come!

It was hard to wait so long. They had waited for him a long time, and their fathers and grandfathers had waited for him too. Sometimes word would go around that he had finally arrived, and in great excitement some of the Jews would get ready to drive the Romans out of Palestine. But always it turned out to be a mistake, and the Jews would be disappointed, and shake their heads, and say, "Will he ever come?"

But when they grew discouraged, they would remember what was written in their Holy Scriptures. For it was surely written there that the Messiah would come someday. There could be no mistake about it. Someday he would come!

And so it went on, month after month, year after year. The people worked, and dreamed, and hoped, and prayed. The rains would fall in October and soften the hard, dry ground after the heat of summer, so that the farmer could do his plowing. And as he plowed the land, the farmer thought about the Messiah, and wondered if he would come before the harvest in the spring. Then spring would come, and the wheat and barley would be growing up in the smiling fields, and all down the hillside the grapevines and the olive trees would be full of fruit. The Romans were still marching through the country, and still there was no Messiah. But the farmer thought that maybe he would come before the next fall rains.

The fisherman would go sailing across the deep-blue Sea of Galilee, and while he waited for the fish to come into his net, he thought of how long Israel had waited for the Messiah to come. The beggars in the city streets, who were deaf, or blind, or crippled, would sit at the corners and ask for money to buy food. They were wondering too if the Messiah would ever come and help the poor folk of Israel.

The shepherds, out on the rocky hills where nothing would grow but grass for sheep and goats and cattle, were also thinking of the Messiah. In good weather and bad they were there, keeping an eye on their sheep, and they had plenty of time to think. When the rain and the snow were in their faces, the shepherds were thinking, *When will he come?* And when the hot sun climbed overhead, and the heat was like a furnace, or when the east wind came and blew dust in their faces, then too the shepherds thought, *When will he come and save us?*

Farmers, fishermen, shepherds—these were not the only people who were thinking of the Messiah. Sometimes along the hot, lonely roads of Palestine, where robbers and wild animals were hiding, a traveler would have dreams. Or the dream might come to someone in sunny Galilee, where camel caravans crossed with their loads of spices and jewels and precious things from Far Eastern lands. But it was most likely to come to a man when he was standing in the great, white, gleaming Temple at Jerusalem, where all good Jews went to worship God.

And the dream would be that the sky opened, and a great light blazed down from heaven. An army came marching down out of the sky, led by a shining warrior whose face was bright as lightning. From his eyes shot flames of fire. His arms and feet shone like polished brass or gold, and when he spoke his voice was like the shouting of ten thousand men. It was King Messiah! "Destroy the Romans!" he would cry. "Burn up their armies! Let not a single one escape!" Fire would pour down from the skies when he gave the

order, and the Romans would melt away to nothing, as though they had never been.

Then the dream would fade away. The dreamer would just be trudging along the dusty road, or watching the camel caravans go by, or standing in the Temple with the crowds of unhappy people pushing all around him.

It was just a dream. The Romans were still there. There was no Messiah anywhere to be seen.

If only the King would come!

2. A King Is Born

NOBODY saw the lions in the daytime, for they were sleeping in their caves. But at night they might come out to prowl around the rocky hills, looking for a fat sheep to eat. After dark the hyenas and jackals began to howl. Robbers might be somewhere in the darkness too. In the night, when other folk were fast asleep, a good shepherd needed to be awake and on the watch, to see that no harm came to his sheep and lambs.

One night when winter was in the air, some shepherds were huddled together on a stony field not far from the town of Bethlehem. Not many miles to the north lay Jerusalem, the capital city of Palestine. But here in the fields it was quiet, and lonely, and cold.

The shepherds sat upon the rocks, or stood leaning upon their staves. Now and again one of them would see something move, or hear a little rustling sound. He would raise his eyes and peer out anxiously into the darkness to make sure that all was well.

Suddenly, without any warning, the sky was flooded with light from beyond the clouds. Everything had been dark a minute before, but now every stone and tree and hillock in the field showed up bright as day.

The shepherds jumped to their feet. Some were too frightened to speak, and others cried out in terror.

"What is it?"

"What can it be?"

"It's the glory of the Lord," one called out. "Lord, have mercy upon us!"

Suddenly they heard a loud, clear voice.

"Shepherds!"

Silence fell upon the group.

"Shepherds, do not be afraid. I bring you the good news which all the Jews have waited so long to hear. This very day, Christ your Saviour has been born in the city of David. And this is how you will know him: you will find him as a baby, wrapped in swaddling clothes, and lying in a manger."

The voice broke off, and a great chorus began to
sing. The sky rang with the music, and these were the
words of the song:

"Glory to God in the highest,
  And on earth peace, good will toward men."

As quickly as they had come, the light and the singing were gone. There was just the darkness again, and
the far-off howling of wild beasts. Everything was the
same as before, except that the shepherds' eyes were
still blinded by the light, and their ears were full of
the music.

18

Their excited voices broke the spell as they all talked at once.

"He's come at last—the Messiah's come!"

"Where did the angel say?"

"The city of David—that means Bethlehem."

"Why are we waiting here? Let's go to Bethlehem."

"Yes, let's go to Bethlehem at once, and find out what has happened there."

For the first time in their lives, the shepherds left their sheep to look after themselves. Across the hills and the stone fences and the rocky fields the shepherds scrambled, and hardly stopped for breath till they reached the edge of the town. Everything in Bethlehem was dark as night can be. But no—not everything. One tiny speck of light was flickering in the blackness.

"He must be where the light is," said one of the shepherds.

Down the street they ran, and in through a door.

They were standing in a stable. There were no angels there. Instead of that, the shepherds saw cows and donkeys eating hay. A cold draft of air was blowing in around the cracks of the door and over the dirt floor. Beside one of the mangers they saw a man standing. A young woman was resting close by. She was watching a baby who lay in the straw.

"We came to see the Messiah," one of the shepherds stammered.

The baby cried. The animals munched their food.

There was some explaining to do. The shepherds told the story of what had happened in the field.

The young man beside the manger did not have anything very exciting to tell the shepherds.

"My name," he said, "is Joseph. This is my wife Mary. We used to live here in Bethlehem, but no one remembers us now. I've been working in Galilee for years. I have a carpenter shop there. The only reason we came back to Bethlehem was to have our names entered in the government records.

"We got here only yesterday. We tried to get a room in the inn, but there wasn't any room for us with all the important people here. They said we could sleep in the stable. The baby came tonight. Here he is, if you would like to see him."

The shepherds looked at the baby. They hoped that they would see something unusual about him, but he looked just like any other baby.

Then they remembered the angels' song.

Outside again, the shepherds looked up and saw a faint gray light streaking the blackness in the east. Morning was coming. Soon the people of the countryside would be getting up.

What a story the shepherds were going to tell them! Who would have thought of looking for the Messiah in a manger! The shepherds were the first to learn the secret. As they walked back to their flocks they prayed and gave thanks to God.

Meanwhile, the little family in the stable were gathered in silence around the manger. Mary, the mother, said never a word, but her thoughts were busy with the tale the shepherds had told about her little child.

The shepherds were not the only people to see strange lights in the sky. Many miles away, three men saw a new star. They were Wise Men, and they knew all the stars, but this one they had never seen before.

It was not only a new star, but a moving star. Like a bright fingertip in the heavens, it seemed to beckon them on. The Wise Men were rich and important, and thought nothing of a journey. At once they made ready and set out to see where the star would lead them. For many days they traveled across the desert, and at last they came to Jerusalem.

Although they were not Jews, they had heard that a Messiah was expected someday in Palestine. When they saw that the star had brought them to Jerusalem, they decided that the Messiah must have come.

"We are strangers here," they said to each other. "We had better ask our way."

King Herod was in Jerusalem just then, and the Wise Men went to his palace. Since they were rich and famous, they had no trouble getting in to see the king.

They bowed down respectfully before the king, and Herod received them with courtesy. Then the Wise Men asked:

"Where is the newborn King of the Jews? We have
seen his star in the east. We have come to worship
him, but we do not know where he is."

Herod was surprised, and then he was angry. A new king of the Jews? Why, Herod himself was the king of the Jews! However, he hid his feelings, and answered,

"I will find out what you want to know."

He left the Wise Men, and hurried off to consult with his advisers.

"The Messiah!" he shouted. "Where do they say the Messiah will be born?"

Solemnly he was told:

"In Bethlehem. An ancient book of the Holy Scriptures tells us that out of Bethlehem shall come a governor to rule the people of Israel."

Fear and jealousy boiled up in Herod. But a king must control his feelings, and Herod was old and wise. When he had called his three visitors to him, he was as smooth and polite as ever. He told them that they would find the child in Bethlehem.

"Go there," Herod said, "and look for him carefully. And when you have found him come and tell me, for I too want to go and worship him."

The Wise Men thanked the king, and set out for Bethlehem. Soon they arrived at the place where Joseph and Mary were staying with the baby. It was very different from Herod's palace.

There the three Wise Men fell down on their knees as they would before a king. They opened their treasures and put their gifts in front of the baby. One brought gold. The others brought sweet-smelling ointments, frankincense and myrrh.

24

"Hail, Messiah!" they murmured in adoration. "Hail, Christ! Hail, King of the Jews!"

When they were once more outside on the road, one of them spoke:

"I think," he said, "that it would be well for us not to see anything of Herod again. I had a dream . . ."

The others agreed with him quickly. They had had a dream too.

"God sent that dream to warn us that Herod is dangerous," they said. "Herod means to harm the child. Let us find some other road back home."

The days went by, and soon the baby was given his name. He was to be called Jesus.

One day, when Jesus was about six weeks old, Joseph said to Mary:

"Now that we have a child, we must go up to the Temple in Jerusalem and give an offering to the Lord. We cannot afford a lamb. But we can at least take pigeons or a pair of turtledoves."

So Joseph and Mary left Bethlehem, and carried Jesus with them to Jerusalem, five miles away.

An old man came up to them in the Temple.

"My name is Simeon," he said. "I have been waiting for you a long time. All my life I have been waiting to see the Messiah. And now the day has come."

He took Jesus from his mother's arms, and as he held the baby he began to pray.

"Lord, let me now die in peace," he prayed. "For I have seen the Messiah, the Saviour of all nations and the glory of the Jewish people."

Simeon turned back to Joseph and Mary, who were looking at him in wonder.

"Mary," he said, "this child of yours is going to break your heart. He will make enemies, and cause great trouble in this country. He will suffer, and others will suffer too, because of him. But also he will give joy, and bring many people to God. God bless you now."

With these words the old man handed the baby back to Mary, and turned away. Joseph and Mary never saw him again, but they remembered his words forever after.

They took Jesus, and started on their walk back to Bethlehem. There was so much for them to think about.

First there was the story of the shepherds. Then the Wise Men had come with their wonderful gifts. And now there was this old man with his strange words of blessing and warning.

Everything seemed to tell them that Jesus was the

Messiah. They should be happier than anyone in the world. And yet they were not happy. There was trouble in the air. Their baby was going to be King of the Jews. Why should there be any trouble about it? They could not understand.

Trouble was not long in coming. One night Joseph had a dream. When he awoke he called to his wife, and told her that they must leave Bethlehem at once. God had sent the dream as a warning for them to get out of the country. They did not dare to stay there any longer. So Joseph and Mary packed up their belongings, and set out for the far country of Egypt where they would be safe.

They left Bethlehem none too soon. For Herod was exceedingly angry when the Wise Men did not come back. Now he was sure that the Messiah really had been born! He was afraid that soon there would be a new king in Palestine to take his throne away from him.

When Herod was afraid, he never wasted any time. Somewhere in Bethlehem was a child whom he feared, and somehow that child must be killed. But he did not know which child it was. How could he be sure to find the right one? He thought of a simple plan.

He called his army officers together, and gave them their orders.

"Send your soldiers to Bethlehem," he told them, "and have them kill every boy in the place who is two years old or younger."

The officers sent their men to Bethlehem, and all the little boys they could find there were put to death. No matter who they were they had to die. It did not take the soldiers very long.

In a few hours they were back in Jerusalem. Herod breathed more easily.

That's a good thing, he thought. *If every little boy in Bethlehem is dead, the Messiah must be dead along with the rest.*

Herod did not know that the baby whom he feared was gone from Bethlehem before the soldiers got there. While the fathers and mothers of Bethlehem were crying because their little ones were dead, Joseph and Mary and Jesus were safely on their way to Egypt.

Herod did not live long enough to find out his mistake. After he died, the little family in Egypt learned that it was safe to go home again.

But this time they did not go back to Bethlehem. They went straight to the town of Nazareth in Galilee, where Joseph had worked before Jesus was born. There they settled down as though nothing unusual had happened.

In Galilee nobody knew that anything strange had happened at all. Nobody there had heard of the shepherds and the Wise Men, and nobody knew what Simeon had said in the Temple. Nobody knew why it was that so many babies in Bethlehem had been murdered. Nobody in Nazareth thought that the Messiah had come.

In Nazareth people only said, "I hear the carpenter
has a son." When Jesus began to walk perhaps they
said, "Joseph's son is strong for his age." And later
they said, "The carpenter's lad is doing well at school."

But there were more interesting things to talk about
in Nazareth than the carpenter's family. There was
the Messiah to talk about. "When will he come?" the
people asked each other.

Nobody in Nazareth had heard the angels sing.

3. Growing

WHEN BOYS in Nazareth were about six years old, it was time for them to go to school. No girls were there, for the girls stayed home with their mothers. But every day except the Sabbath, the boys went to the school and sat on the floor with their legs crossed, and there the teacher taught them many things that every Jewish boy would need to know.

He taught them their A B C's in the Hebrew language. Instead of A, he showed them how to make a mark like this: א. Instead of B, they learned to make this letter: ב; and so on, through all the alphabet. Then when they knew their letters, they could learn to read. And every Jewish boy had first of all to read the Scriptures.

The teacher taught them what was in the Scriptures. Over and over they said their lessons aloud, talking all at once, until they knew everything they were supposed to know by heart.

The teacher taught them psalms which had been sung for many years in the Temple of Jerusalem.

He taught them also about the prophets. The prophets were preachers whose words had long ago been written down in the sacred Scriptures. These books were long pieces of skin, which were kept rolled up when no one was reading them. There were many prophets—Isaiah, Jeremiah, Ezekiel, Amos, Malachi, and many others. Little by little the boys began to discover what these preachers had said.

The teacher also made sure that they knew about that part of the Scriptures called the Law. The Ten Commandments were in the Law, and many other sayings which told people what they must do and what they must not do in order to please God. The boys learned how God gave the Commandments to

Moses, while lightning flashed and thunder crashed, at the far-off mountain of Sinai.

The teacher told them stories of all that had happened to the Jewish people in the years gone by. But the most important was the story of the Passover. This story explained why their parents went to Jerusalem each spring.

Now this was what every Jewish boy had to learn about the Passover, and remember always:

Once there was a time, hundreds of years before, when the Jews did not live in Palestine. They lived in Egypt, where they were slaves. They wanted to escape, so that they might have a country of their own where they could be free.

One spring night God sent a disease into Egypt, and thousands died of it. There was not an Egyptian home where the oldest child in the family did not die. But none of the Jews died. Therefore, they said that God *passed over* their doors that night.

Then there was a great uproar and clamor in Egypt, with the Egyptians weeping, and nursing their sick, and burying their dead. The time had come for the Jews to get away. Under their leader, Moses, they began their long journey toward Palestine.

The Jewish people never forgot what God did for them in Egypt. So in the spring of each year was held the Feast of the Passover, to give thanks to God for the help he had given them long ago. They gathered together and sang:

"O give thanks unto the Lord, for he is good:
For his mercy endureth for ever."

To the Passover feast every family brought a lamb to be killed as a sacrifice to God. Only the best could be given to God. They chose a lamb that was white, and pure, and fine, and precious. Then they roasted the lamb, and ate it. What a feast they had, so solemn and so joyful, as they remembered all that God had done!

Everyone knew the best place to hold the Passover feast was at Jerusalem. Therefore, every year, when spring came round, the people said to one another, "It is Passover time," and as many as could leave their homes went up to the great city.

When the boys heard the story, they understood why their parents went there in the spring.

When Jewish boys were twelve years old, and could read the Hebrew language, and knew the psalms, and understood the prophets, and were learning to obey the Law—then they were practically grown up. At this age a boy could be called "a son of the Law." He could go along with his parents to Jerusalem when it was Passover time.

Each year Joseph and Mary liked to be in Jerusalem for the Passover. When Jesus was twelve years old, he was "a son of the Law," like other boys his age, and for the first time he went with them. Many friends and relatives kept them company as they started on the road.

Now from Nazareth it was more than eighty miles to Jerusalem, and eighty miles is a long way to walk.

It would have been easier to ride in a cart; but nobody traveled that way in Palestine. The roads were too rough and narrow for anything but walking. Donkeys and horses might carry the heavy luggage, but the people went on foot. There were no bridges, and so the only way to get from one side of a river to the other was to find a shallow place and wade across.

It would take two or three days to go from Nazareth to Jerusalem. When the travelers were tired at night, there was not likely to be any place to sleep along the road, except under the open sky and the stars.

There were three stages to their journey. The first was the pleasant part, through Galilee. When the

travelers left Nazareth that day, the sky was clear
and the air was fresh. The fields lay lovely in the sunlight. The roads were full of people from many countries. There were always merchants on the road traveling from the East to Greece and Egypt, and back to
the East again. Galilee was beautiful, and Galilee was
busy.

Sooner or later the time must come to leave pleasant Galilee behind. But which way would they go
from there? Should they go straight south through
Samaria? That would have been the shortest and the
easiest way. The only thing against it was that the
people of Samaria were not friendly to Jews. Long
years before, Samaria had been the home of many of
the Jewish people. But foreigners came and settled
among them. Then their ways became so different
that the people of Jerusalem said they were not Jewish any more. They were bitter rivals of the Jews, and
it was hardly safe to go among them.

So the travelers chose, for the second stage of their
journey, the long road down the valley of the river
Jordan. But they did not find this very pleasant,
either. High above the river stood the banks, and it
seemed as though the river itself were at the bottom
of a great, deep ditch. And down there was the road
they had to take. In some places they came to slime
and mud, and dead trees and twisted roots. But sometimes there were farms and villages. It was hot at the
north end of the Jordan, when first they came to it;

and the farther south the travelers went, the hotter grew the weather.

Very hot, very tired, and very thirsty, they finally reached the last stretch of the journey—across country from the Jordan to Jerusalem. They were nearly there. But the last part of the trip was the hardest of all. Around them stretched a dreary desert. There were bleak hills, and ugly rocks, and hardly a drop of water anywhere to drink. No wonder nobody went to Jerusalem, except Jews and Roman soldiers! There were no gay caravans of Eastern merchants here. Galilee seemed very far away.

Up one side of a hill, and down another, and then another higher hill to climb! Up and up, over stones and bare earth and bushes and thorns, until they were high above the Jordan—that was the road to Jerusalem. Would they ever get there? What they would have given just to sit down and wash the sand off their hot, tired feet!

Then all at once they saw it. From the top of the hill they saw it, walls and roofs and towers gleaming in the morning sun. A shout of joy went up. Every man and woman and child joined in the shouting. Jerusalem, the city of David! King David built that city, a thousand years ago. The enemies of God had come and burned it to the ground, but the Jews built it up again. They were sure that it could never be destroyed. It would always be there, for ever and ever. Someday the Messiah would come, and all the peoples

and nations of the world would come to see Jerusalem, as these poor folk from Galilee were doing now.

The travelers began to march again, but faster this
time; forgotten were the weary miles behind. They
marched, and as they marched they sang. They sang
one of the psalms that the boys had learned at school.
Everyone took up the song:

"'I was glad when they said unto me,
   Let us go into the house of the Lord.
   Our feet shall stand within thy gates, O Jerusa-
      lem. . . .
   Pray for the peace of Jerusalem:
   They shall prosper that love thee.'"

There were so many visitors in Jerusalem that they could not all find a place to stay in the city. Some of them stayed in the villages near by, and others slept in tents out in the open air. At an ordinary time of the year, there would be only about thirty thousand people living in Jerusalem. But at the Passover there might be twice that, or even more.

Even the Roman governor was in Jerusalem at Passover time. He lived in another city, but he always came to Jerusalem for the great feast. It was not that he cared about the Passover. It was because he was afraid that with such great crowds in Jerusalem there might be trouble unless his Roman soldiers were on guard. It would be especially bad if anyone showed up claiming to be the Messiah. All the people might make him king, and rebel against Rome, and great numbers would be killed.

With such crowds in the city, it was hard for the people from Nazareth to get through the narrow streets. All along the streets they saw shops. Some of the shopkeepers were selling goods that had been brought down from Galilee—fish and oil and wine and fruit. Besides the merchants there were shoemakers, butchers, carpenters, tailors. On the side streets goldsmiths and jewelers were making things for the rich people. Here and there was a merchant selling fine silks which had been brought from the Far East. A man could buy almost anything he wanted in Jerusalem, provided that he had the money.

The travelers from Galilee pushed their way through the crowded streets, and on up to the Temple on the hill. Here was God's own house! How large it was! Herod the Great had built this Temple. Ten thousand men had worked many years to build it, and it was not quite finished yet. Eight gates led into the beautiful building with the white walls and the golden towers. Inside there was room for many thousands of people.

What a clatter and a clamor and a tumult there was! It seemed as though all the world were there. Doves and cattle, as well as lambs, were offered in the Temple as a sacrifice to God. You could hear the poor creatures calling out—the cows lowing, the lambs bleating, the doves singing their sweet, sad song. Money was clinking on the tables. Only one kind of coin could be used as an offering, and travelers had to exchange those they were carrying for Jewish money. The men who made the exchange often cheated the visitors.

The people from Galilee separated when they came to the Court of the Women. The women and girls could go no farther, but the men and boys went up some steps into the Court of Israel. There they watched the priests of the Temple taking the doves and lambs and cattle that the worshipers had brought, and offering them up as a sacrifice. The priests killed the animals, and let the blood drip on the altar where the sacrifices were given to God.

The Court of Israel was as far as anyone could go, unless he were a priest. There was another room called the Holy Place, which only priests could enter. To the people it was a place of great mystery. Then farther on was a still more mysterious room called the Holy of Holies. Even a priest did not dare to step inside that door. That was the secret place of God. Only the high priest, who was head of all the priests, could enter there. And he could go in only once a year.

The visitors from Nazareth saw a priest coming toward them. Anyone could tell from his clothes that he was wealthy. He came from one of the families that were known as the Sadducees. The Sadducees were the only people who were at all friendly with the Romans. The reason for this was that they were better off than most other people and well-satisfied with things as they were. They thought it wise to stay on good terms with Caesar. Nobody liked the Sadducees very well, but everyone had to admit that they were certainly very important. They sat in a high council and governed everything that went on around the Temple.

And here was a Pharisee, looking very well pleased with himself! Jesus had seen Pharisees before, around Nazareth, and they always seemed to have that look. The word "Pharisee" meant "someone who is different." What made the Pharisees different was that they were always talking about the Law, and claiming that they obeyed it better than anyone else. They were kindly folk, on the whole, and very well respected, but they did not have any official position, like the Sadducees. All they did was study the Law and tell other people about it. The Pharisee whom the visitors were watching began to pray so that everyone could see him. It seemed as if he were saying, "O Lord, I thank thee that I am better than these other people here!"

Most of the great throng crowding the Temple were not priests, or Sadducees, or Pharisees. They were plain people who had come to bring their sacrifices, or to talk about the Scriptures, or simply to be in the Temple because they loved God's house.

Nobody was paying much attention to Jesus. He was just a young boy, lost in the crowd.

The days went by, and the lambs were killed and eaten. The prayers were said and the hymns were sung. It was all over at last, and the time had come to go home.

Joseph and Mary did not see Jesus the morning they all were supposed to leave. They did not wait to find him, for the other travelers from Nazareth were anxious to get started on the long journey back to Galilee.

Joseph and Mary said to each other:

"Jesus is safe enough. There are so many of us from Nazareth that he can't get lost. No doubt he is somewhere in the party."

The Nazareth people said good-by to the Temple for another year, and started off for home. Out through the city gates they went, and back into the desert through which they had come. They walked a whole day, and still Joseph and Mary saw no sign of Jesus. This was beginning to seem strange. Surely they would see him somewhere!

At last it dawned upon them. He wasn't there at all!

They were frightened now. What could have happened to Jesus? What would become of him in Jerusalem? There was nothing to do but to leave the party, and turn back alone to the city. But Jerusalem was a big place, and they hardly knew where to hunt for Jesus. How would they ever find one boy among all those thousands of people?

They went to the Temple. But even if he were here, it would not be easy to find him quickly. Walking through one of the courts, they noticed a group of people gathered around a rabbi. There was nothing unusual about that. There were a great many teachers in the Temple, and a visitor often saw groups gathered around them to listen to their teaching.

But there was something different about this group. Most of the men in it were Pharisees who were themselves rabbis. And the strange thing was that they were not doing all the talking as they usually did. They were listening too. And they were not listening to a rabbi, but to the voice of a boy.

45

Joseph and Mary moved closer. There could be no mistake about it—it was Jesus who was talking! He was asking questions; he was answering questions. The long-bearded rabbis were standing there, their mouths open in astonishment. Jesus was not just a boy in the crowd any longer. Men old enough to be his grandfather were listening to what he had to say.

Mary's surprise turned to anger. She pushed her way through the crowd and took Jesus by the arm.

"Why did you do this?" she cried. "Your father and I have been looking for you everywhere."

Jesus stood just where he was. It was as though he belonged there. He said:

"Why did you come to look for me? Don't you know that I must be looking after my Father's business?"

Joseph and Mary stood there too, not knowing what to make of their boy or of what he said.

They waited to see what he would do.

And then, in a minute, Jesus turned and went with them. They did not have to ask him again. The three of them went home to Nazareth.

Jesus knew that someday he would go back to the Temple. But he was not ready for that yet. He must do his duty to his parents. He must obey God at home. Then he would always know how to obey God in the wide world beyond Nazareth.

The lambs went quietly to the Temple when they were taken there to be offered to the God of Israel. Jesus must be obedient like a Lamb of God.

4. Jesus Goes to Work

WHEN JESUS was thirty years old, people began to talk about the great man who had come to Palestine.

"This man is so great," they said, "that he may be the Messiah."

But it was not Jesus they were talking about. It was his cousin, John.

John was a preacher. He was afraid of no one, and as a result everyone was a bit afraid of him. John was a rough, strong man. Next to his skin he wore leather, and over that he wore a cloak of camel's hair. Honey and locusts were his food.

Every day John preached down by the river Jordan. The people flocked out from Jerusalem and from all the countryside round about to hear him preach. It was a wild and dreary place to come to, but when John preached everybody wanted to be there.

This was how he preached:

"Give up your sins, and begin a new life at once, for God is coming to rule over men! I am a voice crying in the wilderness. I tell you—prepare for the Lord!"

And when the people heard him, they were afraid. Many of them cried out, "We have sinned!" and came forward out of the crowd. John led them down the bank into the river and baptized them as a sign that they wanted to be cleansed of their sins and begin a new life. Thus John came to be known as "John the Baptist."

But when John thought that a man was not in earnest, then he refused to baptize him. Some of the Pharisees and the Sadducees came to be baptized, and John would have nothing to do with them. They might be great men in Jerusalem, but John called them "snakes in the grass." He told them:

"I've seen the snakes out here in the wilderness,

wriggling for dear life to get out of the way when the grass catches fire. That's what you remind me of. You're scared. You think that something terrible is going to happen, and so you're pretending to be good people so that it won't go so hard with you. You will have to show me that you want to be something different from what you are! And don't think that you amount to anything just because you are Jews. God could make as good Jews as you are out of these stones."

That is how John the Baptist talked to some of the great men of Jerusalem. It made people think more than ever that he might be the Messiah. Who except the Messiah would dare to talk that way to Pharisees and Sadducees?

But others shook their heads and said, "No—this couldn't be the Messiah!" For they thought that when the Messiah came he would drive the Romans out of the country; and many people said that the only way to do that would be to get an army together. Some men were meantime killing all the Romans they could. They were called "Zealots," because they were so much filled with zeal about killing off the Romans. A few even carried daggers with them, and stuck the daggers into Romans whenever they got a chance.

"The Romans will not be overthrown," they said, "just by preaching. You will have to get out and kill the Romans."

John himself said that he was not the Messiah.

"There is someone coming who is greater than I," he told the people. "Someone is coming whose shoelaces I am not worthy to stoop down and untie. Compared to him, I am nobody. I am just preparing the way for the Messiah."

One day there was a great crowd, as usual, down by the Jordan, and John was busy baptizing the people as fast as they came to the water. One after another they came. It went on for hours.

John had just baptized one man and helped him to the bank. The next one was coming forward. John looked up to see who it was. He was looking into the face of Jesus of Nazareth.

"You! Not you!" John spoke in a hoarse whisper. "No! I can't baptize you. You must baptize *me* instead!"

Before anyone could notice that anything was wrong, Jesus stepped to the water's edge.

"Don't say anything about it, John," he said softly. "Treat me just like the rest of them. We shall all be baptized together into a new life."

Jesus went forward into the river and John baptized him. In a moment Jesus was up the bank and lost in the crowd. The next man was coming forward.

John stared after the vanishing figure of Jesus. The crowd made way for Jesus, thinking, *There goes another man who came to be cleansed of his sins.*

But John said: "When I baptized *him*, I saw the Spirit of God come down out of heaven like a dove, and light upon him. Jesus is the Son of God. I am nothing. He is everything. He is the Messiah. He is the Lamb of God!"

The next man was coming down the bank toward John. John stood peering into the crowd. Jesus was nowhere to be seen.

Jesus had gone away to be alone, as God wanted him to do. He went into the loneliest part of the desert, where there were only the wild animals to keep him company.

I am the Messiah, he thought. *There is no doubt that I am the Messiah. I must save my people. How should I begin?*

There was nothing to eat in the wilderness, and Jesus grew hungry. He looked around him, and saw that the stones were shaped like loaves of bread.

There seemed to be a voice inside him which was not his own. The voice said:

"If you really are the Messiah, you oughtn't to be hungry. If you really are the Messiah, you would just have to say the word and these stones would be turned into bread. Then you would have plenty to eat for yourself, and, besides, you could go and give bread to all the hungry folk out there who are waiting for you to help them."

It was very quiet in the wilderness. The voice spoke up again.

"But maybe you are afraid to try. Suppose you said to the stones, 'Stones, become bread!' and then nothing happened! That would prove that you weren't the Messiah, wouldn't it?"

Jesus shook his head, to get rid of the thought. Some words from the Scriptures came into his mind. *"Man shall not live by bread alone, but by every word that proceedeth out of the mouth of God."* No, it would not do to try playing tricks with stones. It would not matter if he did turn them into bread. Bread was not the most important thing in the world. People might think that there was nothing so important as eating, but there were bigger things in life than that. People might think that what the Messiah ought to do was to make the country prosperous, but that would not help them so much as they thought. That was not the kind of Messiah he was going to be.

But what was the best way to prove that he was the Messiah? The tempting voice inside tried again.

"Maybe the best idea," it said, *"is to go to Jerusalem and climb up on the tower and jump down! Everyone says that the Messiah is going to come suddenly out of heaven. You would come down suddenly enough that way! And nothing would happen to you. It says in the Scriptures that God will send his angels to hold you up and keep you from being hurt. Surprise the whole city by jumping off the Temple, and everybody will worship you at once!"*

Again Jesus shook the thought away, and again he thought of what the Scriptures said.

"Thou shalt not tempt the Lord thy God." *I can't go and put God to the test, to see whether he will keep me from being hurt. And it won't make me the Messiah just to cause a big sensation in Jerusalem. That's what everyone is expecting, but that is not the right way at all. There must be some other way.*

And the voice spoke up again.

"There is something else you could do. What the world

needs is a ruler like you. Everybody says that the Messiah is going to be a world ruler, great and good. Don't let the people down! You are a great man. You could be anything you wanted to be—a general, a governor, a king."

Jesus thought, *That's Satan tempting me, that's the devil himself talking!*

He spoke out loud:

"Go away from me, Satan! For the Scriptures say, 'Thou shalt worship the Lord thy God, and him only shalt thou serve!'"

The voice said no more. A great quietness came over Jesus. There was no great thing that he needed to do right away. He was the Messiah, but he did not need to make the country wealthy. He did not need to jump from the Temple, and he did not need to command an army or rule an empire.

There was one thing that he would have to do, but he could not tell anybody about it yet. It was going to be his secret for a while. But someday everybody would see what he was doing. Someday it would be understood.

And now it was time to be on his way. He had been in the wilderness forty days, and that was long enough. He found the trail back to the outside world, and soon he was on the road to Galilee.

When Jesus got home to Galilee, he began to preach to people in the streets. What he said at first was very much like what John the Baptist said:

"Give up your sins, and begin to live a new life, for God has come to rule over you!"

But the crowds that heard Jesus were not so large as those that went to the Jordan to hear John.

Jesus needed some followers now who would be with him all the time, and learn everything he had to tell them. John the Baptist had his followers; "disciples" was what they were called. Jesus began to look for disciples of his own.

One morning he went down to the shore of the Sea of Galilee. When he came back to the town, he had four disciples with him.

Two of them were brothers named Simon and Andrew. Andrew remembered Jesus, for he had once been a disciple of John the Baptist. He had seen John point to Jesus, and heard him say, "He is the Lamb of God!" Andrew had told Simon all about it.

When Jesus came to them along the shore of the Sea of Galilee, he found them putting a net into the water, for Andrew and Simon were fishermen.

Jesus said to them,

"Come and follow me, and I will make you fishers of men."

Fishing was good business, but Simon and Andrew were ready to give it up to follow the man John had called "the Lamb of God." They came away with him at once.

Farther along the shore was another pair of brothers. One of them had also been with John the Baptist. Their names were James and John, and they were with their father, Zebedee. They had done so well at fishing that they could afford to have servants to help them. But when Jesus called them they also came at once, and left their father and the servants behind.

That was four to start with, and soon he had eight others. But no one of them was a very important person, and people said that one of them was wicked. That was Levi, who was also called Matthew. The trouble with Levi was that he was a taxgatherer. Everybody hated taxgatherers. They were called "publicans," and it was thought that no one could be much lower than a publican.

The publicans worked for the Roman government. They were not Romans themselves, but Jews, which made it all the worse. They were looked upon as traitors, for they collected the taxes for the hated Romans, and made a fortune for themselves by cheating the people.

Levi's job was to collect the fee for traveling along the road, and what he could collect over and above the amount he ought to have charged, he kept for himself. Then Levi heard Jesus preaching. He heard him say that he ought to give up his sins, and begin to live a new life. When Jesus came to Levi's table one day, and said, "Follow me," just as he had said it to the honest fishermen by the lake shore, Levi was ready to come away. Without a word Levi got up and left his taxgathering behind, and all his fortune. Levi became a disciple like the other eleven, and was treated like the rest.

But other people were shocked when they saw a publican with Jesus, and tongues began to wag. No one seemed to notice that Levi had stopped collecting taxes. He had been a publican once, and no one except Jesus was ready to give him a second chance.

Other publicans sometimes came to have dinner with Jesus and his disciples, along with many people who were looked down upon in the community.

The Pharisees in particular were angry when they saw the company that Jesus kept. One day they came to one of these dinner parties, and told the disciples that they did not care for Jesus' choice of friends.

"How is it," they asked, "that your master eats and drinks with publicans and sinners?"

Jesus heard them, and replied:

"It is not well people who need a doctor, but the sick. I didn't come here for the sake of the good people, such as you think that you are, but for the sake of sinners—to lead them into a new life."

But the Pharisees still objected. They said:

"Look at John the Baptist. John is a good man. His disciples are so religious that they sometimes go without their meals. Your disciples always seem to be eating!"

"Why shouldn't they eat and feast and be merry?" Jesus answered. "They are like the friends of a man who is being married. When someone is to be married, his friends have a great feast. They are joyful because the bridegroom is with them. In the same way my disciples are joyful because they have me with them."

Jesus meant that they were joyful because he was the Messiah, and his disciples were glad to be with him. But he did not say that he was the Messiah, and no one knew what he was talking about. The Pharisees would have had more respect for him if he had had a better class of friends. Fishermen might do, but not publicans and sinners of that sort! If only Jesus were more like John the Baptist!

They never once thought that Jesus might be the Messiah. When they saw the kind of friends he had, they wondered if he was even a good man.

5. A Busy Time

THE PHARISEES may not have liked Jesus, but no one could deny that he knew how to preach. The crowds that came to hear him were growing larger. Often Jesus stood at the foot of a hill and preached to the crowd that had gathered on the hillside.

Now everyone who heard Jesus preach was likely to be surprised. For he did not say the things that people expected to hear. Often he said the very opposite of what they wanted him to say.

He did not believe in giving people a good opinion of themselves. He told them what was wrong with them. He did not say that it was easy to be good. He said that it was much harder than anybody thought. He did not try to preach sermons that would make him popular, for he was not thinking of himself. He was thinking of what God had to say to the people, and so he told them plainly what they ought to know and what they ought to do.

Jesus knew that his listeners found it easier to hate other people than to love them. And so he stood one day at the foot of the hill and said:

"You have all heard the saying, Love your friend and hate your enemy. But that is not what I say. I say, Love your enemies, bless those who curse you, and pray for those who use you badly. That is what God does. He makes the sun rise on everybody, good or bad. He sends the rain to fall on everyone, no matter who he is.

"If you love only those who love you, you don't deserve any credit for that. That's what everybody does. Be like God. He is merciful, and you ought to be merciful too. Forgive those who do you a wrong, or you cannot expect God to forgive you."

All the people thought that they were at least doing the right thing in hating the Romans. How could anyone help hating those rough Roman soldiers, who often came along and made Jews carry their packs for them? But Jesus said,

"If a Roman soldier makes you carry his pack for a mile, carry it another mile as well, to show that you love him."

Another thing that Jesus knew about his listeners was that many of them were worried about money, and food and clothes. It was hard to blame them for that; for some of the people were very poor, and were never sure that they were going to get enough to eat.

Jesus was poor enough himself. His disciples were also poor, and they got no richer by following him.

Turning to the disciples, Jesus said to them,

"Blessed are you who have nothing you can call your own."

The disciples pricked up their ears. "Blessed"— that meant to be fortunate, or well off. What was good about having nothing? Jesus went on:

"Blessed are you who have nothing, for yours is the kingdom of heaven.

"Blessed are you who often go hungry, you shall be fed later on.

"Blessed are you who are sad, the time will come when you will be joyful.

"Blessed are you, when other people hate you, and will have nothing to do with you, because you are my disciples. Be glad when that happens, because that is what has happened to all God's servants. God will reward you for everything you suffer for my sake."

There was silence. Jesus looked out over the crowd and spoke again,

"Woe to you who are rich!"

Again the disciples were amazed. The rich people would not like that! The disciples were poor themselves, but they wondered what was wrong with being rich.

Jesus thought of a rich man whom he knew, who wore fine purple clothes and ate the best food in the land. And he thought of a poor beggar who sat all day long outside the rich man's house. His body was covered with sores, and he was so hungry that he would have been glad to get the crumbs that fell from the rich man's table. But the only friends he had were the dogs that came and licked his sores.

Jesus continued, in a stern voice:

"Woe to you who are rich! For you have already had everything you are ever going to have! Woe to you who are well-fed! The time is coming when you will go hungry. Woe to you who are enjoying yourselves all the time! Someday you will weep. Woe to you when everyone speaks well of you! It is easy to be popular if you aren't faithful to God. That's the way it has always been."

Jesus knew that all of them were too much interested in the things that money could buy. They wanted the Messiah to come so that he would make them all rich. And so Jesus said, to show them where they were wrong:

"Don't be always thinking about what you are going to eat and drink and wear. Why, that's the kind of thing the Romans worry about. There is more to life than food and clothing."

He paused for a moment. It was a warm summer day. The birds were flying overhead, and singing; and up the hillside the wild flowers made patches of color in the grass. Jesus spoke again:

"Look at the birds of the air. They never plant crops, or reap harvests, or gather the grain into barns. Yet your Heavenly Father feeds them. Are you not more important than birds? Think of the lilies of the field, how they grow. They never yet made any clothes for themselves, and yet the great King Solomon in all his glory was not so beautifully clothed as one of these little flowers. You people who have so little faith in God—think! If God clothes the flowers of the field, which are here today and gone tomorrow, will he not clothe you? Seek the Kingdom of God first of all, and you will be given all the food and clothes you need. Never worry about tomorrow. Tomorrow will look after itself when it comes. Think about how you ought to live today."

There was another weakness that Jesus had seen in people, especially in the Pharisees. They loved to show off their good deeds. He had to speak about this too.

"When you give something to the poor," he said, "don't make a great noise about it, like some people I could mention, who want to impress everybody with how generous they are. If you give anything, keep quiet about it. God will know what you have done, and that's enough.

"It's the same with prayer," Jesus continued. "Don't stand praying on the street corners where everyone can see you. There are many people who do that. When you pray, go into your own room and

pray with the door closed. God will hear you, and he is the only one who needs to hear."

Jesus had his admirers. Some people admired him so much that they began to call him "Master" and "Lord." But Jesus did not think that they were all in earnest. He spoke plainly about this also.

"It won't do you any good to come saying, 'Lord, Lord,'" he said, "unless you do the things God expects of you. Someday, I suppose you will come and tell me of all the wonderful things you have done in my name. And then I will have to say to you: 'I don't even know who you are. Go away!'

"If anyone hears my teachings, and does what I tell him to do, he will be like a man who builds his house upon a rock. The rain comes down and the wind blows, and the house keeps on standing there, because it is built upon a rock. You will be strong like that house, if you do as I say. But anyone who hears my teachings and pays no attention to them is like a man who builds his house upon the sand. When the rains and the floods and the winds come, the house will fall down and that will be the end of it. You will be weak like that house, if you do not obey my words."

Now when the people heard how Jesus preached, they were amazed. They wondered who this was who spoke to them as though he were God himself. That was not how other preachers taught. They were always quoting somebody else, as though they were afraid to speak for themselves.

But Jesus simply said, "*I* am telling you." He said, "Listen to *me*."

Every Friday evening at sunset the Sabbath began, and there could be no more work until sunset on the following day. Saturday morning all the Jewish people went to attend the service in the synagogue. The people would come in and take their places, with the most important people up in front. At the beginning of the service, everyone stood and faced in the direction of Jerusalem, and recited some verses from the Scriptures. These were always the same. They began: "Hear, O Israel: The Lord our God is one Lord: And thou shalt love the Lord thy God with all thine heart, and with all thy soul, and with all thy might."

After this there was prayer. Then the minister opened a cabinet and brought out the Scriptures, which were written on long pieces of skin made into a kind of paper. The pieces were kept rolled up when they were not in use. The minister brought two of the rolls and laid them on the reading desk. Someone read the Scripture lessons then, and after that anyone in the congregation who wished could go up to the front and explain what the lesson meant.

Like all the other Jews, Jesus went to the synagogue on Saturday mornings. One Saturday when he and his disciples were in the town of Capernaum they went to the service as usual. When the time came to explain the lesson, Jesus went up to the front. He surprised the people as he always did; but something else happened which surprised them even more.

There was suddenly a great commotion at the back of the synagogue. A man began to cry out. There seemed to be some evil thing inside him, which made him hate the very sight of Jesus. The people said that he had "an unclean spirit."

Strange, wild words came pouring out of the man's mouth.

"Let me alone!" he cried. "What have I to do with you, Jesus of Nazareth? Have you come to destroy me? I know who you are. You are the Holy One of God!"

Jesus stood his ground, and spoke to the evil thing in the man.

"Be quiet," Jesus said, "and come out of that man."

There was another wild shriek and then silence. The man looked around him as though he wondered where he was. He was in his right mind again.

The people were amazed by what they had seen and heard. On the way home from the synagogue they asked each other,

"What kind of preaching is this, which makes a madman well again?"

Before the day was over, word of what Jesus had done had gone all over town.

After the service, Jesus went to Simon's house, and there he found more trouble waiting for him. Simon's wife's mother was sick in bed. Jesus went to her bedside, and took her hand, and helped her to her feet. All at once the sickness left her, and she was able to prepare the meal.

Jesus could rest in the afternoon, but when the sun went down in the evening he had to go to work again. Everyone had heard of how he cured people who were out of their minds, and of how he was able to heal the sick. As long as the Sabbath lasted, the people had to stay quietly at home. But once the sun had set the Sabbath was over, and they could do as they pleased. It seemed as though the whole town wanted to do only one thing, and that was to go to see Jesus.

A great throng of sick people were soon gathered outside the door of the house, with everyone else in Capernaum looking on. Jesus came out to heal the sick. Darkness fell, and night came on, and still the people pressed around Jesus to have him touch them and make them well. Hour after hour he worked with them, until it was too late to do anything more that night.

Yet Jesus was out of bed in the morning before the sun was up. It had been a busy Sabbath, and he needed to go off by himself and rest. And what he needed more than anything else was to pray. He wanted to be alone for a while with his Father. So many people to preach to! So many men who had begun to hate him! Jesus needed strength for it all, and he knew that praying would make him strong.

While everyone else was sleeping, and the darkness still lay upon the land, Jesus silently slipped away from the house. He found a lonely place, where no one would disturb him.

But when Simon and the other disciples woke up, they could not wait for him to come back. They went at once to look for him. And when they had found him, they said,

"Everyone is looking for you."

It was quiet out there in the hills. Jesus would have liked to stay there for the whole day. All day long he could have rested and prayed. But then he thought of the people who were waiting for him. He thought of the people who needed him. He thought of the places he had not yet visited. There was so much to do, and there was so little time.

He rose to his feet.

"Let us go, then," he said. "Let us go to the next towns, so that I can preach in them too. After all, that is why I came into the world—to tell men the good news from God!"

He left the quiet countryside, and went back to the towns. The people who loved him were there. The people who needed him were there. And the people who were afraid of him, and the people who had begun to hate him—they too were there.

Jesus returned to the towns, where his friends and his foes were waiting.

6. Friends and Foes

JESUS THOUGHT the time had come to visit Nazareth. Before he had gone away, there was nobody who thought that he was a person of any great importance. But he had become a famous man. The whole of Galilee was talking about him. And now he was at home with his friends and family again.

On the Sabbath morning he went to the old familiar synagogue. There was a full congregation that day, for everyone supposed that Jesus would preach. He had never preached in Nazareth before.

When the time came to read the Scripture lesson, Jesus walked up to the front. He took the roll from the minister, and found the place he wanted. It was in the book of the Prophet Isaiah. He began to read:

"The Spirit of the Lord is upon me, because he has anointed me to preach good news to the poor; he has sent me to heal the broken-hearted, to preach liberty to the prisoners and recovering of sight to the blind, to set free those who suffer, and to say that God will be good to his people."

Jesus stopped reading and handed the roll back to the minister. He sat down in the seat from which Jewish preachers always spoke to the people in the synagogue.

The whole congregation was very still, waiting to hear what Jesus had to say. That was an exciting lesson he had read from the Scriptures. It made the people think of the Messiah. Someday a preacher would be able to say, "This has all come true!" And that would mean that the Messiah had come.

Jesus looked around at the faces he knew so well. Thirty years he had lived among these people. Now he was back to tell them something that they had never known before.

He began to speak.

"Today," he said, "you are seeing this Scripture lesson come true."

A thrill ran through the audience. The Scripture had come true? The Messiah was really here? Could

he mean that *he* was the Messiah? The people gasped. Some laughed. Others were angry. They started to talk among themselves.

"The Messiah? Him? Why, that's only Jesus! The carpenter's son!"

"Everybody knows who Jesus is! Lived down the street since I don't know when!"

"Who does he think he is?"

Jesus again raised his voice above the others':

"I know what you are going to say. You are going to quote that old saying, 'Doctor, cure yourself.' You are going to tell me to start doing the things I am supposed to have done in Capernaum. I'm not surprised. A servant of God never gets any honor among his own people. The same thing happened to the prophets long ago.

"Don't expect me to do anything wonderful here in Nazareth. You wouldn't believe it if you saw it. Why do you think you ought to get any special favors from God?"

A great roar went up from the congregation. All his old friends got up from their seats and rushed to the front of the synagogue. They took hold of Jesus and dragged him out of the building. At the edge of the town there was a high cliff, and they took him there to throw him down on the rocks below. But Jesus slipped out of their hands, and turned around. Calmly he walked through the crowd. Nobody had the courage to touch him again.

Jesus never went back to Nazareth any more. Once, when he was preaching in another town, someone came and told him that his mother and his brothers had come to take him home. They thought that he ought to stop this nonsense of pretending to be the Messiah.

But Jesus would not go home with them, for they did not believe in him. It was better to stay with his disciples. He was at home with those who trusted him.

"My mother?" he said. "My brothers?"

He looked around at his disciples, and said: "These are my mother and brothers—my own disciples. Anybody who obeys the will of God is my brother and my sister and my mother, all in one. That's the kind of family I want!"

Back in Nazareth nobody thought that Jesus was of much account. But in other places he meant everything to people who needed help. The Pharisees were often glad to see him go away. But the poor and the sick could never see enough of him.

Once there came to Jesus a man who was sick with the dreaded leprosy. A leper's skin was deathly white, and his flesh was rotting, and he was sure to die of the disease. Nobody needed help more than a leper did, but no one would even touch him.

The people back in Nazareth were too proud to admit that the carpenter's son from down the street

might be the Messiah. But a leper did not have any pride. This leper came to Jesus, and fell on his face before him, crying out, "Lord, if you will do it, you can make me clean from this disease!"

Then Jesus did what everybody else was afraid to do. He reached down and put his hand on the sick man, and said:

"I will. Be clean."

At once the man was healed of his leprosy. Jesus told him to go and give thanks to God, and not to tell anyone what had happened. But the leper could not help telling. Jesus became still more famous as the man who healed the sick.

Another time he made a blind man see again. The Pharisees tried to get this man to say that the person who cured him had not been sent from God. But the man who had been blind knew better. When the Pharisees tried to threaten him, he did not give an inch. He said:

"Who ever heard of anyone opening the eyes of the blind since the world began? But this man did it. How could he have made me see, if he hadn't come from God?"

When Jesus heard of this, he went and found the man who had been blind, and asked him,

"Do you believe that I am the Son of God?"

The man answered,

"Yes, Lord, I believe."

The blind man had found his Messiah.

Then there was a man who was paralyzed so that he could not move. His friends wanted to bring him to Jesus, but there were so many people standing around the house where Jesus was teaching that they could not get near him. But somehow or other they must get the sick man there.

Like many of the houses in Palestine, this house had a flat roof, with a stairway leading up to it. They placed their friend on a mat, carried him up the stairs, and cut a hole in the roof. After fastening a rope to each corner of the mat, they gently lowered it to the floor, right at Jesus' feet.

Jesus was glad when he saw the faith they had in him. He looked at the helpless man, and said,

"Man, your sins are forgiven you."

There were scribes and Pharisees standing there, waiting, as usual, to find fault with Jesus. They began to talk among themselves. They said:

"Who is this who is talking as if he were God? Such blasphemy! Who can forgive sins, except God himself?"

But Jesus knew what they were saying, and he answered them:

"Which do you think is easier—to say, 'Your sins are forgiven you,' or to say to this man, 'Pick up your mat and walk away'? I will show you that I can do one as well as the other!"

He turned to the paralyzed man and said,

"Pick up your mat, and go on back to your house."

The sick man got up from the floor, rolled up the mat and put it under his arm, and went home. As he walked, there was a song of praise to God in his heart. And many of the people who saw what had happened were so surprised that they did not know whether to be glad or to be afraid. But they all agreed on one thing. They said,

"We have seen strange things today!"

Nothing that Jesus did seemed to please the Pharisees. But there was one thing that made them especially angry. He was not so careful as they thought he ought to be about keeping the Law.

Now the Law meant everything to the Pharisees. They were so much in earnest about keeping God's Law that they were not satisfied with what was in the Scriptures. They followed many rules which had been made up since the Scriptures were written. Unless a man kept all these rules, it did not matter to the Pharisees how much good he did.

Jesus was always getting into trouble with them about the Sabbath. The Pharisees had a list of thirty-nine different kinds of work that nobody was allowed to do on the Sabbath Day. This list included so much that unless a Jew was careful, he would be likely to break the Sabbath without even knowing it.

If he tied a knot that could be untied with one hand, that was all right; but if he took two hands to untie it, then he had broken the Sabbath. He even had to be careful about sitting in a chair, for if he happened to drag his chair across the dirt floor the Pharisees said that he was plowing, which was a great sin on the Sabbath Day. It was forbidden to make a fire on the Sabbath. And so, if a woman wanted hot food, she had to cook it the day before, and keep it warm. But that did not mean that she could set it on a stove. For the stove might get hotter than it was, and make the food hotter, and that was just the same as making a fire.

The only safe way to keep a meal hot was to wrap the dishes in cloth or pigeon feathers.

Jesus did not think that rules like this were what the Scriptures meant when they said, "Remember the sabbath day, to keep it holy." He did not think that this was the way to honor God. And because Jesus did not agree with them about the Sabbath, the Pharisees were always watching for a chance to put him in the wrong.

Once, when Jesus and his disciples were walking through a field of grain on the Sabbath Day, the Pharisees saw that the disciples were eating some of the grain. There was nothing wrong with eating it, if they were hungry. But the trouble was that in order to get the grain they had to pluck the ears. That, said the Pharisees, was harvesting! Moreover, they had to take the ripe ears and rub them in their hands to get rid of the chaff. The Pharisees thought that that was just the same as threshing! Such things to do on the Sabbath Day! The Pharisees stopped the disciples, and demanded to know why they were doing something that was against the Law.

It was really Jesus with whom they wanted to pick a quarrel, and so Jesus answered for the disciples:

"Why, you must have read in the Scriptures that King David and his soldiers once went into the Temple and ate some of the holy bread which only a priest is allowed to eat. Surely if David could do a thing like that, my disciples can pick a few ears of grain in a field!

"You don't understand what the Sabbath is for," Jesus went on. "We aren't supposed to be slaves to the Sabbath; this day is meant to do us good. The Sabbath was made for man; man was not made for the Sabbath."

Then he added something else, which took the Pharisees by surprise:

"The Son of man is Lord also of the Sabbath."

They were puzzled. Jesus was talking again as though he was the Messiah. So far as the Pharisees could see, Jesus was just a preacher who broke the Law.

The Pharisees began to watch him still more carefully. They found another chance to get him into trouble soon after this. Jesus had gone into the synagogue to teach, and in the synagogue was a man whose hand was withered and useless. On any other day there was no doubt that Jesus would heal this man. But this was the Sabbath, and it was against the Law to heal anybody on that day unless he were in danger of dying. A man with a withered hand could wait another day.

Surely even Jesus would not dare to break the rules again!

Jesus knew that they were watching to see what he would do. They would never forgive him if he made a move to heal this man.

He called out to the man,

"Stand up—up here, in front of everybody!"

When the man had come to the front, Jesus turned to the Pharisees.

"I am going to ask you something," he said. "If any one of you owned a sheep, and it fell into a pit on the Sabbath, wouldn't you lift it out? And don't you think that a man is worth more than a sheep? You say that it is against the Law to heal a man on the Sabbath. *I* say that it is *always* right to do good to somebody, on the Sabbath just the same as any other day!"

He looked around at the whole crowd. He was angry now. Would they actually let a man suffer one day more than was necessary? He turned back to the man with the useless hand.

"Stretch out your hand!" he commanded.

And when he spoke, the withered hand was healed, and made as good as the other one.

The Pharisees went out of the synagogue, and their faces were hard with anger.

"He has gone too far!" they said to one another.

"He is breaking all our good rules. It is not safe for the country to have him around. He ought to die!"

They really meant it. They thought they were doing the right thing. They were afraid of what Jesus would do. The Pharisees even called in some of their enemies to ask their advice about the best way to get rid of Jesus.

Meanwhile Jesus had gone out of the city to be alone again. On a lonely mountain, under the moonlight, he prayed to his Father all night long. Back in the city men were planning to take his life. And out on the mountain Jesus prayed for power to do good to men.

7. Slow to Understand

NOT ALL the Pharisees treated Jesus as an enemy. There was one of them, named Simon, who decided to have Jesus come to his house for dinner.

Perhaps Simon thought that the other Pharisees were too hard on Jesus. Perhaps he thought that he might show Jesus where he was wrong. Or perhaps he was just curious. Jesus had become very well known, and many people called him "Rabbi" or "Teacher." It would be interesting to talk with the famous rabbi all afternoon.

Whatever the reason was, Simon asked Jesus to come and have a meal with him and his friends.

While they were eating their dinner, a woman stole in quietly through the open door. She had not been invited. Simon would never have dreamed of inviting her into his house, for everyone in town gave her a bad name. "She's not a good woman—not a nice woman at all," people said. They turned their eyes away when they met her on the street.

At any other time the woman would not have wanted to come to Simon's home, for no one likes to be stared at coldly and be put out of the house. But today was different. Jesus was there.

She brought with her a box of ointment. Ointment was the gift that Jewish people brought, when they wanted to honor an important person or some dear friend.

Clutching her box of ointment, the woman crept across the room to where Jesus was sitting. She began to cry. The tears rolled down her cheeks and dropped on Jesus' hot, dusty feet. Then she wiped his feet with her hair and kissed them. She opened her precious box and began to rub his feet with the soft white salve.

No one spoke or moved. Simon was angry and disappointed with Jesus. The other Pharisees were right after all!

So this is the great new prophet, sent from God! he thought to himself. *If Jesus were a prophet, we shouldn't be looking at a scene like this. He would know what kind of woman that is who is touching him. Why, everybody knows how bad she is!*

Jesus did not need to be told what Simon was thinking. Still sitting there, while the woman clung to his feet, Jesus spoke.

"Simon, I have something to say to you."

"Yes, Rabbi?" Simon replied. "What is it?"

"Let me tell you a story," Jesus said. "There was once a moneylender who had two men owing him money. One of them owed him five hundred dollars, the other owed him fifty. Neither of them had anything with which to pay him back, so the moneylender told them both to forget about the debt—that they didn't need to pay. Now tell me—which of those two men will love the moneylender most?"

Simon answered,

"Why, I suppose the man who owed him the most."

"That's right," Jesus replied. "Now, Simon," he went on, "look at this woman. When I came to your house today, you didn't even give me any water to wash the sand off my feet, though that is what is done in friendly homes. But this woman has washed my feet with her own tears, and dried them with the hair of her head. You have scarcely been polite to me; but this woman has done nothing but kiss my feet. You never thought of putting ordinary olive oil on my head; but this woman has put precious ointment on my feet.

"You think this woman is a great sinner," Jesus continued, "and so she is. She has done many things that are wrong. But her sins have been forgiven her.

I have brought her to a new life, and she doesn't have to worry any more about the sins of the past. That is why she loves me so much. But, of course, a person who hasn't had his sins forgiven isn't going to know much about love."

Jesus turned away from Simon. He might have added:

"A cold Pharisee like you, so sure that nothing is wrong with you, is a great deal worse off than this poor, sinful woman. You have got all your sins still to worry about, and you don't even know it!"

But Jesus did not say it. He left Simon to think that out for himself. Instead, he spoke to the woman,

"Your sins are forgiven."

The other people in the room began to mutter to themselves:

"There he goes—forgiving sins again! What right has he to forgive anybody's sins?"

But Jesus paid no attention. He spoke once more to the woman at his feet:

"Your faith in me has saved you," he said. "Everything is all right now. Go in peace."

That was the end of the dinner party at Simon's house. But it was not the end of the talk and gossip about the kind of friends that Jesus made. Some thought he must be bad himself because he had so much to do with people to whom the Pharisees would not even speak. Everywhere he went, there was the same complaint.

Time and time again Jesus tried to explain why he was more interested in sinners than in anyone else. Why, the people that the Pharisees despised were the very people who needed his love the most! What could be better than to save somebody from an evil life?

Jesus told story after story, to show the Pharisees what he meant. One time he said:

"Suppose a shepherd had a hundred sheep, and one sheep strayed away from the others and got lost. Would he not leave the other ninety-nine, and go after the lost sheep until he found it? And when he did find it, he would pick it up and carry it joyfully home. Then he would go around and tell all his friends and neighbors. He would say: 'Rejoice with me! For I have found my sheep that was lost.'

"Or suppose a woman had ten silver coins, and dropped one of them on the floor. Wouldn't she light a candle and sweep the floor and look everywhere until she found it? Then she would say to her friends and neighbors: 'Rejoice with me! For I have found the coin that I lost!'

"In the same way," Jesus said, "God is more pleased over one sinful person who stops sinning than over all the others who think they have never sinned."

The Pharisees still did not get the point. So Jesus tried again with another story. He said:

"A certain man had two sons. One day the younger son said, 'Father, give me my share of the property which is coming to me.' So the father gave each of the sons his share.

"Then the younger son packed up his belongings, and went away to a far country. There he spent all his money foolishly. After his money was gone, this young man had nothing left to live on. He went to work for a farmer, who sent him out to feed the pigs. He was so hungry that he would have been glad to eat the pigs' food, but no one gave him anything.

"Then one day he said to himself: 'What a fool I am! Why am I staying here?' He thought of how even the servants at home had plenty to eat, while he was starving to death. He said: 'I will go back to my father, and tell him that I have sinned against him and against God. I will tell him that I am not worthy to be his son, and ask him to give me work as one of his servants.'

"So he went home. But before he reached the house, his father saw him coming, and ran out to welcome him. The young man started to say, 'I have sinned, and I am not worthy to be your son.' But his father called out to a servant: 'Bring the best clothes in the house, and shoes for my boy's feet. Then kill the fattest calf we have, and get a feast ready. My son is back, and we are going to celebrate!'

"Meanwhile, the older brother was out in the field. When he came home, he heard music and dancing in the house. He asked a servant why they were having a party. When he was told, he became very angry.

He would not even go into the house. When his father came out to ask him to join the party, the older brother said: 'All these years I have stayed at home and helped you! I did everything you told me to. In all that time you never once gave me a party. But when my brother comes back from spending your money— why, nothing is too good for him!'

"But the father answered him kindly. 'Son,' he said, 'you are always with me, and everything I have is yours. It is right that we should celebrate, and be happy. For it is as if your brother had been dead, and now he is alive again. He was lost, and now he is found.'"

The days went by. Some days were good, and some were bad. Once in a while Jesus would find somebody who seemed to understand him and believe in him. Then again it would seem that he was failing in what he tried to do.

The time he healed the Roman officer's servant was one of the good days. Jesus was just coming back to Capernaum after preaching out in the country, when this officer approached him. Although he was a Roman, and the captain of a company of Roman soldiers, this man was well liked in Capernaum. For he had built the Jews a synagogue, and everyone knew that he loved the Jewish people.

He came to Jesus, and said, "Lord, my servant is lying at home, very sick and suffering greatly."

Jesus replied at once, "I will come and heal him."

But the officer shook his head.

"Lord," he said, "I am not worthy that you should come into my house. Just speak a word, standing here, and that will heal my servant. You see, I have an army under me. I say to a soldier, 'Come here,' and he comes. I tell my servant to do something, and he does it right away. You have that kind of power too. You just have to say that my servant shall be healed, and he *will* be healed."

Jesus was joyful when he heard these words. To those who were standing around he said:

"I tell you, I have not found among the Jewish people anyone who believes in me so much as this Roman does! And I tell you this too: When you talk about the Kingdom of God you shouldn't think that God has no place in it for anyone except Jews. God is going to bring together people from every country, everybody who has faith like this officer's faith. And some of the Jews may find themselves outside the Kingdom looking in!"

Then he turned to the officer and said:

"Go back to your house. You have had faith in me, and I will give you what you ask."

When the officer went home, he found that his servant had recovered from his illness while Jesus was speaking.

That was one of the good days, when Jesus found a new believer. But a bad day came, when Jesus found that his oldest friend had begun to lose faith in him. John the Baptist was not sure any longer that Jesus was the Messiah.

And John was in trouble. He had preached against King Herod, the son of the king who had died when Jesus was a baby. Herod married another man's wife, and John the Baptist said that this was a sin. Herod threw John into jail.

As John lay in his prison cell day after day, he began to wonder about Jesus. Had he been wrong in thinking that Jesus was the Messiah? Jesus did not seem to have done very much as yet. The Romans were still in the country. The rich people were as bad as they had always been, and the poor were just as poor.

At last John could not stand it any longer. When two of his followers visited him in jail, he sent them to ask Jesus who he really was.

"Ask him," said John, "'Are you or are you not the Messiah?'"

John's followers found Jesus busy healing the sick. They drew him aside, and told him what John wanted to know.

"Are you the One who was to come," they asked, "or must we look for somebody else?"

So even John the Baptist had his doubts! John, the man who had said that he was not worthy to baptize

Jesus; the same John who once called Jesus the Lamb
of God!

Jesus pointed to the crowd of people whom he had
been healing, and he said to John's disciples:

"Go back and tell John what you have seen and
heard here. Tell him I am doing what I can. Tell him
how the blind are getting back their sight. Tell him
too, how the lame are learning to walk, and how the
lepers are being cured. Tell him that I am preaching
to the poor. Tell him all about what I am doing, and
let him decide for himself whether or not I am the
Messiah. And tell him this: Blessed is anyone who
believes in me, and takes me just as I am!"

Jesus never heard what John thought of this message. For John did not live much longer. One night King Herod gave a birthday party, and a pretty girl danced so well that the king offered to give her anything she asked. The girl went to her mother, to find out what she ought to say. Her mother hated John the Baptist because he had spoken the truth, and so she told her daughter:

"Ask for the head of John the Baptist to be brought in here on a platter!"

The girl went to the king, and asked for John's head. The king was sorry then that he had made that promise, for he was half afraid of John. However, he had to keep his word. And so he sent servants to the prison, and they cut off the head of John the Baptist with a sword, and brought it back to the palace on a platter.

When Jesus heard what had happened, he felt very sad. He said,

"Let us go out to some quiet place, and rest awhile."

Things were not going very well. John the Baptist was dead, and Herod might be planning to kill Jesus next. Some men, in fact, came one day to warn him to get out of Herod's kingdom.

"Go and tell that fox," he said, "that I am busy curing the sick and conquering evil, and neither Herod nor anybody else is going to stop me until I have finished my work!"

But things were going badly, just the same. Jesus saw that there were not many of the people who understood his message or knew who he was. A few believed in him, but others soon lost interest in him, if they ever cared at all. Only once in a long while did he see any results from all his work.

He explained this in one of his stories when he said:

"A farmer went out to sow his seed. As he sowed, some of the seed fell in the pathway, and people walked on it, or the birds ate it up. Some fell on a rock, and this seed began to grow; but no sooner had it sprung up than it died, because it did not have deep roots. Some fell among thornbushes; and the thorns grew faster than the seed, and choked it. But some of the seed fell on good ground, and there it grew into a good harvest."

When the disciples were alone with him, they asked Jesus to tell them what this story meant. He said that the seed stood for the words that he spoke to them. Some people heard him, but they soon forgot what he said. That was like seed falling on the pathway.

Others were very excited about what he said when they first heard it, but when it was hard to do what he told them they soon gave up trying. That was like seed falling on a rock, where there was no soil or water to give it root.

Then there were some who cared more about money and pleasure than they cared about God. That was like seed being choked by thorns.

But some people heard Jesus preach; and they believed in him, with good and honest hearts, and they were faithful. That was when his preaching brought results, and it was like seed falling on good rich earth.

"Unless people have faith in me," said Jesus, "they will never understand God. They will see the things I do, and never even know what they are looking at. They will listen to me, and never know what they are hearing. I can do nothing with them. But you—my disciples—you have faith in me. You will understand everything someday."

The disciples were going to be good ground for the seed that Jesus sowed.

8. Jesus Is Strong

THAT NIGHT Jesus said to the disciples, "Let us go across the lake."

Simon and Andrew and James and John were fishermen. They knew where to get a boat, and they knew how to sail it too.

All twelve disciples, along with Jesus, climbed into a boat and pushed away from shore.

The Sea of Galilee was a lovely blue lake in the daytime, when the sunlight sparkled on the water. In the evening it was lovely too, when the waves were lapping peacefully against the side of a boat, and the stars came out twinkling overhead.

But the Sea of Galilee was not always so lovely or so peaceful. Sometimes the wind came roaring down the steep banks around the lake, and the water grew white and angry.

Then again everything might be calm and quiet when a boat left the land. But before it had gone very far a storm might be howling all around. It would toss the boat around like driftwood, and then it would be too late to turn back to shore.

107

Some of the disciples were fishermen, and they had fished here all their lives. They knew what the sudden storms were like. It was no surprise to them when the stars disappeared as though the rising wind had blown them out. They knew what was coming now. The night would grow black as ink, and the great foaming waves would smash against the ship and fill it up with water. There was nothing anyone could do about it. Nobody could sail or row or steer the boat any longer. Only God himself could bring the poor sailors safe to shore.

The sea was rough already, and getting rougher every minute. They were afraid. They were always afraid of the sea when storms began to blow. It was so big and dangerous and terrible, and men were so small and weak! It was like a frightful monster, tossing them up and down before it swallowed them alive.

If only they had stayed on the good, safe land! They had been so worried and so tired that night; so discouraged about Jesus and his work. And now there was this storm on top of everything! It looked as if none of them would live to see another day. They had left their homes and families behind, to follow Jesus. What was the use of following Jesus if they were all to be drowned?

Now the boat was full of water. They tried to bail it out, but the fishermen knew that nothing they could do would be of any use.

In the dark they could hardly see one another's

faces. Where was Jesus? No one had heard a word from him since the storm began to blow.

They found him at the back of the boat, just where he was when they left the shore. He was stretched out on a seat, resting on a pillow. And he was fast asleep!

The disciples were angry. Any minute now the boat was going to turn over, and there was Jesus sleeping as though nothing in the world were wrong!

One of the men took Jesus by the shoulders, and shook him awake. They shouted at him, "Master, doesn't it matter to you if we are all drowned?"

Jesus rose to his feet in the tossing boat. The wind blew in his face, and he seemed to be answering it. The sea smashed against the boat again, and Jesus cried out, "Peace, be still!"

All at once the wind began to die away. The waves tossed for a minute or two longer, but not so strongly now. Everything was growing quiet. The stars began to shine again, and soon there was no sound but the water lapping gently against the boat.

Jesus spoke to the disciples:

"Why were you so frightened? How is it that you still haven't any faith in me?"

But the disciples scarcely noticed what he was saying. They were more afraid than ever. This time it was not the sea that frightened them. They were afraid of Jesus. They said to one another:

"What kind of man is this? When he speaks, even the wind and the sea obey him!"

In the morning they brought their little boat to land on the other side of the lake. Over here in the country of the Gadarenes, Galilee seemed very far away.

A high cliff rose above the sea. Jesus and the disciples climbed up and looked around. There was nothing much to see except some men feeding a herd of pigs. In the distance was a graveyard.

Suddenly a man came running out of the graveyard. He was naked, and his body was covered with cuts and bruises. The man was out of his mind, and he lived by himself in the graveyard, and wandered through the mountains. Other people had often tried to chain him up, but he was so strong that he broke the chains as if they were made of string. He could be heard crying out, day and night, and he was always cutting himself with sharp stones. No one dared to go near him.

The madman ran toward Jesus, shouting at him. His words were like those of the other madman who had interrupted Jesus in the synagogue service.

"What have I to do with you, Jesus? What have I to do with the Son of the most high God? Don't torment me!"

Jesus said to him, "What is your name?"

The man answered: "My name is Legion. There's a whole legion of devils inside me!"

The disciples were meanwhile listening in horror. There was something evil in this man, something as dreadful as the storm of the night before. They heard Jesus say: "Come out of the man!" Then they seemed to hear many voices crying out, and calling to Jesus, and pleading with him. And they heard Jesus say, "Go!"

The wild look left the man's eyes. And at that very moment the pigs went wild. The man was in his right mind now, but it seemed as though the pigs had gone crazy. With a great snorting and squealing they ran to the cliff and plunged into the sea.

After that everything was quiet. It was as quiet as it had been when Jesus stilled the storm. The evil thing was gone. The morning sun was shining brightly on a peaceful countryside. There was nothing dreadful any more.

But what they had seen was too much for the men who had been feeding the pigs. As fast as their legs would take them they ran to the nearest town and told everybody what had happened. The people came flocking out of the town to see for themselves. When they came they found the madman sitting there talking to Jesus. He had put on his clothes, and he was just as sensible as anybody else.

The people had been terribly afraid of the madman, but now they were afraid of Jesus. They had tied this man up with chains, and still they could not hold him. Yet here was a stranger from Galilee who cured the madman with a few words. *What kind of man is this?* they thought. *What kind of power does he have?*

They were so worried about what Jesus might do next that they asked him to leave the country. Without a word Jesus took his disciples back to the boat. The man who had been out of his mind followed him, and asked if he might go along. But Jesus told him:

"No, you have work to do here. Go back home to your friends. Tell them what the Lord has done for you."

The man went back to the city, and began to tell his story. The story went abroad through that whole country, and everyone who heard it was amazed.

For the disciples it had been a night and day of wonders. But as they sailed home across the lake they did not know that an even greater triumph was waiting for Jesus on the other side.

As their boat drew near to land, they saw a crowd standing on the shore. Everyone had been watching anxiously, waiting for Jesus to come.

When Jesus stepped ashore, the waiting crowd made way for a man who was well known in the town. His name was Jairus, and he was the chief officer of the synagogue.

Jairus fell down at Jesus' feet and began to plead with him to come to his house at once:

"My little girl is dying. Please come and put your hands on her, and heal her, and make her live!"

Jesus went with Jairus, and the whole crowd followed to see what he was going to do. As they walked

along the street, with people pressing in on them from every side, Jesus suddenly stopped and said,

"Who touched my clothes?"

The disciples could not imagine what he was talking about. They said to him:

"Why, don't you see the crowd? Everybody is touching you! What do you mean by asking, 'Who touched my clothes?'"

But Jesus answered:

"There's someone in particular who touched me. I felt power going out of me."

With that, a poor woman came out of the crowd and fell down in front of Jesus. She was trembling with fear. She told him her whole story. For twelve years she had been sick. She had spent all her money on doctors, and she never got any better. She thought that if only she could touch his clothes, without anyone seeing her, she would be made well.

Jesus looked at her kindly, and said:

"Your faith has made you well. Go in peace."

Meanwhile Jairus was waiting impatiently for Jesus to come along. Soon it might be too late!

At that very moment a message came from Jairus' house. The worst had happened. The little girl had died, and there was no use troubling Jesus. Already it was too late.

But before Jairus could speak, Jesus took him by the arm and said:

"Don't be afraid. Just keep on believing."

He sent the crowd away, and told the disciples that none of them could come with him except Simon and James and John.

Jairus led the way to his house. When they got there they found that the bad news was true. The little girl had really died. Already the flute players, who played at funerals in Palestine, had arrived. Everyone was mourning and weeping.

Jesus spoke sharply to the mourners.

"Why are you making all this fuss?" he asked. "The little girl isn't dead. She is only sleeping."

Everyone laughed at him, as though he were a fool. "So he doesn't know the difference between being asleep and being dead," they said to themselves. But Jesus told them to get out of the house. When they were gone he took Jairus and his wife, and the three disciples, and went into the little girl's room.

There could be no doubt about it—the girl was dead. She was lying white and cold and still. No doctor in the world could ever help her again.

Jesus bent over the still body, and opened his mouth to speak. Simon and James and John held their breath. Not many hours before, they had heard him say to the sea, "Peace, be still." When he spoke, the sea obeyed him. They heard him speak to a madman, and after he spoke the man was in his right mind again. But what use would it be to speak to someone who was dead? The dead could not hear him!

Or could they hear him? Had Jesus not once told

them, "The dead hear my voice"?

The little girl did not know anything. She did not hear anything. She could not know or hear anything, for she was dead.

Then a voice came through the silence. The little girl began to hear someone talking. It was a man's voice, and it was saying the very words her mother used each morning to wake her up from sleep.

"Little girl, get up!" she heard.

She opened her eyes. She looked into the face of Jesus. He took her hand, and helped her to her feet. Her parents were there too. She went to them.

"Give her something to eat," said Jesus. "And say nothing about what has happened."

But no one could keep a secret like that. Soon everyone had heard the story. Everybody heard how Jesus spoke and brought the dead back to life.

9. Refusing a Crown

UP UNTIL this time, Jesus had done all the preaching, and the disciples had listened. Jesus had healed the sick, and the disciples had watched. Now, however, Jesus told the disciples that it was time for them to work also. He called the twelve together, and said:

"I am going to send you out in my place. You are to divide up into pairs. Each pair will go and preach in the towns and villages. You will tell the people what you have heard me say—that God has come to the earth to rule over men's hearts. When you see

people who are sick or out of their minds, you are to make them well, just as you have seen me do."

He told them plainly what they were to do.

"Don't take any money with you," Jesus said, "and don't ask for money from anybody. Don't take many clothes, either; you are to travel quickly, and attend to your work, without worrying about money or clothes. You will be taken care of."

"When you go into a city or a village, find some family that will welcome a preacher; and stay in that home until you go to the next place. If nobody will listen to you, go somewhere else. But before you go, warn the people in the place which you are leaving that they have sinned by not paying attention to God's message."

So the disciples went out and preached as Jesus told them. They healed the sick, as Jesus did.

The trip was a great success. After many days the
disciples began to come back home, with many stories
about their experiences. When they were all with
Jesus again, they sat down and told him everything
they had said and done.

Jesus listened to their stories, and then he said:

"It is time for you to take a rest. Come with me to
some lonely place where nobody will disturb us for a
while."

They got into their boat, and sailed up to a quiet
place they knew of, near the town of Bethsaida. But
they got no chance to rest after all, for the people at
Capernaum saw them leaving.

"There go Jesus and his disciples!" somebody said. "They're heading for Bethsaida!"

A crowd of people began to walk around the shore of the lake. As they went, others joined them from the towns and countryside round about. Jesus was the most popular man in Galilee just then. Wherever he went, he might be sure that a crowd would follow him.

The people walked and ran, and by hurrying they reached the quiet spot near Bethsaida as soon as Jesus did. When he stepped out of the boat, thousands of people were waiting for him on the shore. Jesus had gone away for a rest, but when he saw the people he felt sorry for them.

They are like a flock of sheep, he thought—*a flock of sheep with no shepherd to look after them.*

They had spoiled his holiday, but Jesus spoke to the people and said that he was glad to see them. Then he began to teach, just as he did in the cities and towns. All day long he taught, and if there were any who were sick, he healed them.

The day wore on, and evening was drawing near. One or two of the disciples pulled Jesus' sleeve, and said to him:

"Master, it is getting late. Hadn't you better send them away to find something to eat in the towns near by? There is nothing for them out here in the country."

Jesus answered: "There is no need for them to go away. Give them something to eat right here!"

The disciples looked at him as if they did not know whether he was serious or not. They said: "Do you mean that you want us to go and buy food for all these people? Where would we get enough money for that?"

Andrew said: "There's a boy here with five loaves of bread and a couple of fishes. But how far will that go among five thousand people?"

Jesus only answered, "Tell them to sit down on the grass."

The disciples went among the crowd, and had the people sit down in groups, fifty in each group.

Jesus took the five loaves and the two fishes, and as he held them, he said a prayer of thanks to God. Then he broke the loaves, and gave the bread and the fish to the disciples and told them to pass the food around among the crowd. They passed it here and they passed it there, but they never ran out of food. Nobody could tell where it was coming from, but there was enough for everyone and some left over.

The people were hungry after their long walk and the hours of standing in the sun. They ate heartily. As they finished their meal, they began to think about what had happened.

"Where did all this food come from?" they began to ask themselves. "Where did Jesus get all that food?" "There were but five loaves and a couple of fishes and yet we have all had enough and to spare!"

The crowd began to talk in excited voices. "Jesus gave us this food." "A wonderful thing! He gave us

food to eat, when there wasn't anything here!" "Why, this is just the man we have been looking for!" "There's the man to make the Jews strong and rich— he makes food out of nothing!"

The people were rising to their feet.

"Make him a king!" they started to cry. "Jesus is the man to be king of the Jews!" they shouted. "We want our king!"

But Jesus was not there any longer. Jesus had gone; he had slipped away through the crowd and disappeared. Even the disciples did not know where he was. He stayed alone in the mountains until long after dark.

Those foolish people! That foolish, foolish crowd! They did not understand him at all. Did they never think of anything except their stomachs?

Jesus remembered how the devil had once tempted him in the wilderness. What was it that the devil had said? "If you are the Messiah, make these stones into bread."

Yes, all the people would be for him so long as he gave them something to eat. They would even make him a king, if they thought he was the man to get rid of the Romans and make the country free and rich and great. Why, they had offered to make Jesus a king that very day! They said that he was just the man they had been waiting for!

But that was not what Jesus had come to do. He did not want to be that kind of king.

It was soon to be Passover time. Many years ago, at Passover time, Jesus had been a boy at the Temple in Jerusalem, watching as the lambs were killed for a sacrifice. A year from now it would be Passover again. And then it would be time to go to Jerusalem once more. He would go to Jerusalem, and he would be the King of the Jews. Then he would do what he always knew that he would have to do someday.

When Jesus came back to Capernaum, he gathered his band of disciples together and took them away again. This time he took them so far away that no one would follow them. No one wanted very much to follow, anyway, for the people were hurt and angry because Jesus would not be their king.

Jesus led the disciples away to the north, into the country near Caesarea Philippi. Here one of the rivers that flowed into the Jordan came springing out of a cave in a hill. Here too the Greek people round about had built temples for their heathen gods.

Jesus wanted to be alone with his disciples, for the time had come to have an important talk. He said to them: "Who do people say that I am?"

The disciples answered: "Some people say that you are John the Baptist, come back from the dead. Others say that you are Elijah, or Jeremiah, or one of the other prophets come back to earth. Everyone thinks that you are a great man."

"But who do *you* say that I am?" Jesus asked.

There was silence. Then Simon spoke up: "You are the Messiah—the Christ—the Son of the living God!"

That was it! That was what Jesus was waiting for! His face lighted up in joy. He turned to Simon, and exclaimed: "That is the best thing that could happen to you, Simon, to find out who I am! And no human being could have told you! Only God himself can have shown you that I really am the Messiah, when nobody else believes it. And now you are going to have a new name, Simon. I am going to call you 'Peter' from now on, for the name 'Peter' means 'The Rock.' You have faith in me, and your faith is like a rock. I am going to build my Church on faith like yours, and nothing shall ever conquer it. It will be the strongest thing in all the world.

"And now"—Jesus began to speak more quietly— "and now that you know who I really am, I have many things to tell you. In the first place, you must not say anything about my being the Messiah—not just yet. And this is more important: I am not going to be very popular any more. I am going up to Jerusalem, and when I get there, my enemies will plot against me and put me to death."

Peter thought that this was nonsense. Everyone knew that the Messiah would not be killed like that, but would instead be a great warrior and a triumphant king. In a bold voice Peter spoke up again: "Don't be foolish. Nothing of that sort is going to happen!"

Jesus turned on Peter. This time he was not joyful; he was angry. He talked to Peter in the same way he had once talked to the devil in the wilderness.

He said: "Get behind me, Satan! The devil has got into you, Peter! God didn't have anything to do with what you said to me just now. You're talking like everybody else. You're weak. A man who tries to save his own life is sure to lose it. But if a man gives up his life because of me—ah, that man will really know what it means to live!"

But Jesus saw that the disciples did not understand. Even Peter was losing his faith again. Somehow he must make them believe in him and trust in him.

So six days later he took Peter and James and John, to whom he showed the most secret things, up into a high mountain. And there the disciples saw a marvelous vision. Jesus' face became bright as the sun, and his clothes shone like the morning light. They said afterward that Moses and Elijah, who were great among the Jews in the days of long ago, came down and talked with Jesus.

Peter spoke timidly this time, for he did not know what to say.

"Lord," he said, "it is good for us to be here. Let us build three tabernacles here, one for you, and one for Moses, and one for Elijah."

Then a great cloud came, like a shadow, over the mountain. They heard a voice from the cloud, like the voice of God, saying: "This is my beloved Son, in whom I am well pleased. Hear him!"

The disciples fell down to the ground, and there they lay until Jesus came and touched them. At his touch they looked up, and there was no one to be seen but Jesus standing there alone.

"Come away," said Jesus, "and tell nobody what you have seen."

They followed him down the mountain, back to where other people were.

Long afterward, they spoke of what had happened. They told of the brightness, and the beauty, and the visitors from olden days, and the voice which said that Jesus was the Son of God. But in those days they never said a word.

They knew that on the mountaintop they had been with God.

10. The Way to Jerusalem

JESUS had made up his mind that he would go to Jerusalem for the Passover next year. He knew that if he did he would get into trouble. The disciples knew it too, for he had told them so. There was a hard time ahead for them all.

There was hardly anyone whom Jesus could count on any more. Often even the disciples did not understand him. Once in a while other people would offer to come along and be disciples too. But few actually came, after Jesus explained how much he expected his disciples to give up for his sake.

There was one man who came to Jesus, and said bravely, "Lord, I will follow you wherever you go!"

Jesus replied: "Even the foxes have holes in the ground to sleep in at night. The birds of the air have their nests. But I travel across the country without a home that I can call my own."

The man thought of his own comfortable house, and decided he did not want to follow Jesus after all.

Another time Jesus invited a man to join him. This man said that he would be glad to come, but that his father had just died, and he must first look after the funeral. That would take a long time, for the Jews loved their customs, and when anybody died they held ceremonies which lasted for many days. Jesus could not wait for this man, so he answered:

"Let people who don't believe in me look after things like that. You have something more important to do. Your job is to go out and preach, right away. That's what you would do if you really believed in me."

Still another man was willing to come, if only he could first go home and say good-by to his family. Jesus saw that this man too had not really decided to give up everything for God. He told him:

"You're like a farmer who starts to plow a field, and then turns around and wonders if he shouldn't be doing something back at the house. Unless you put your whole heart into following me, I'm afraid you will never be of much use."

Even some of those who used to call themselves followers of Jesus were going away. Jesus said to the twelve, who had been with him from the beginning:

"Are you going to leave me too?"

Peter answered: "Lord, where would we go? We should die if we did not hear your words. We believe that you are the Christ."

Jesus said, "Yes, you are the men I have chosen to be with me—though there is one of *you* who will come to a bad end."

He was speaking of a disciple named Judas Iscariot, though the others did not know it. Jesus knew that Judas was not to be trusted.

In those difficult days Jesus spent much of his time in prayer. The disciples felt that they also needed strength and help from God. Once, when Jesus had finished praying, they said to him,

"Lord, teach us to pray, just as John the Baptist used to teach his disciples."

So Jesus taught them a prayer, and this is how it went:

"Our Father, which art in heaven, hallowed be thy name. Thy kingdom come. Thy will be done on earth as it is in heaven. Give us this day our daily bread. And forgive us our debts, as we forgive our debtors. And lead us not into temptation, but deliver us from evil; for thine is the kingdom, and the power, and the glory, for ever. Amen."

Then Jesus looked at his disciples, and told them that they ought to pray more than they did.

"Suppose," he said, "one of you went to a friend's house at midnight, and called through the window, 'Lend me some bread, for company has come unexpectedly and I haven't anything in my house.' Your friend might not want to get up out of bed, but if you kept on pleading with him, he would give you what you asked for. In the same way, keep on praying to God! Prayer is like knocking on a door. Knock, and the door will be opened."

Jesus knew, better than the disciples did themselves, how much they were going to need God's help.

Jesus ran into a great many trying people in the next few months. One day there was a lawyer who thought that he knew more than Jesus did. He wanted an argument which would give him a chance to show how much he knew, so he came and asked Jesus,

"What should I do to have eternal life?"

Jesus answered, "What does it say in the Law?"

The lawyer replied, "It says, 'Thou shalt love the Lord thy God with all thy heart, and with all thy soul, and with all thy strength, and with all thy mind; and thy neighbor as thyself.' "

Jesus said: "That is right. Those are the things you ought to do."

It sounded to the lawyer as though Jesus were saying, "If you knew all along, why did you need to ask me in the first place?" The lawyer thought that he would get the better of Jesus, so he replied,

"Well, just who is the neighbor that I am supposed to love?"

Jesus answered with a story:

"A man was traveling on the lonely road between Jerusalem and Jericho. As so often happens there,

some thieves jumped out of a hiding place, and robbed him and beat him. He was lying there half dead, when a priest from the Temple in Jerusalem came along. He took one look at the wounded man, and kept on going along the other side of the road. Then somebody else from the Temple, who was supposed to be a very religious sort of person, passed by, and the same thing happened.

"Finally a Samaritan came along. I don't need to tell you how Samaritans and Jews hate each other! But this Samaritan was sorry for the wounded man. He put bandages on his wounds, and took him to an inn. Before he left next morning, the Samaritan went to the innkeeper. He paid the bill for the man who had been robbed. Then he told the innkeeper to take care of the man, and the Samaritan said he would pay for

133

anything more that was needed the next time he came.

"Now, think of those three men who passed along the road. Which of them was a real neighbor to the man who was robbed?"

The lawyer said, "Why, the one who helped him, of course."

"Then," said Jesus, "go and do the same."

What Jesus wanted the lawyer to understand was:

"You really know what a good neighbor should be, because God has been good to you. But you are not much interested in being a neighbor to people who need your help."

But if the lawyer did not see that for himself, there was no use telling him. He would be too proud to understand.

Another day there was a man who came to Jesus and said:

"Master, I wish you would speak to my brother. Our father died a little while ago, and my brother is keeping all the property for himself. Make him give me my share of it."

Jesus would have nothing to do with the quarrel. He told this man:

"You ought to think of something besides money and property. There is more to life than owning things. Let me tell you a story.

"There was a farmer whose crops were so good that he had no place to put all the harvest. He said to himself: 'I will pull down my old barns, and build bigger ones, and put my crops in them. Then I will take life easy, for I have enough money to last me for many years.'

"But do you know what happened? That very night God said to him, 'You fool, you are going to die tonight; and what good are your crops and your money going to be to you then?' That's what becomes of people who keep all their money for their own selfish use, and never think about God."

There was another man who was a great disappointment to Jesus. He was a young man—rich, and a leader in the community. He came and kneeled before Jesus, and said,

"Good Master, what should I do in order to have eternal life?"

This was like the lawyer's question, but this man asked it in a different spirit. He really wanted to know.

Jesus answered:

"Do you know what you are saying when you call me 'Good Master'? No one is good except God."

Jesus was wondering if the rich young man knew that he was talking to the Messiah, or if he thought that Jesus was just a man who was a little better than others. However, he went on:

"If you want to have eternal life, keep God's commandments. You know what they are: Do not kill, do not steal, live a pure life, do not tell lies, honor your father and mother, and love your neighbor as yourself."

The young man exclaimed: "But I have kept all those commandments ever since I was a boy! What is it that is wrong with me?"

When Jesus saw that the young man was in earnest, he loved him. He replied:

"There is indeed something wrong with you. It is the way you love your money. Give it away to the poor, and you will be rewarded in heaven. Give up everything you have, and come and follow me."

The young man got slowly to his feet. No! That was asking too much! How could he live without his money? He needed his money. How did he know that God would look after him if he did not take care of himself? Without another word he went away.

"How hard it is," Jesus said, "for rich people to obey God!"

The disciples were amazed. They had always thought that the reason why some people were rich was that God was pleased with the good lives they had been living. They said, "If there isn't any hope even for rich people, is there any hope for *anybody?*"

"No," Jesus replied, "there isn't any hope for anybody. No one is good enough. But God can help and save sinners, whether they are rich or poor. God is everybody's hope."

Peter spoke for the rest of the disciples. He said, "Well, we have given up everything to follow you."

Jesus answered, "If you have given up anything for my sake you will never have reason to be sorry for it, either in this life or after you die."

The months were going by, and it was time to be getting on toward Jerusalem. Jesus took his disciples and crossed to the east side of the river Jordan. They traveled south, and then crossed the Jordan once again and came to the city of Jericho.

In the rich earth around Jericho beautiful gardens grew, and the palm trees stood tall. Travelers who came from the swamps of the Jordan loved to stop at Jericho before they took the hard and lonely road that led to Jerusalem. There were desert lands and hills ahead, but at Jericho there was water to drink, and good food to eat, and a place to stay in comfort. But Jesus could not stay long in Jericho. It was to Jerusalem that he was going, and nothing could hold him back.

The people at Jericho heard that Jesus was passing through their city, and a crowd gathered in the streets to catch a glimpse of him as he went by. There was a man named Zacchaeus there. He was shorter than most other men, and he could not see Jesus because of the crowd around him. There was no use asking anyone to help him, for no one liked Zacchaeus. He was a taxgatherer, as Matthew once had been, and had grown rich collecting taxes. But he had grown unpopular too. The Jews thought him a traitor, for although he was a Jew he worked for the Romans, and made his fortune out of cheating his fellow Jews.

But Zacchaeus was determined not to miss seeing Jesus. Running on ahead of the crowd, he climbed a sycamore tree. High above the street, he could look down at Jesus, but there was no reason to think that Jesus would look up at him.

However, when Jesus reached the place where Zacchaeus was hiding in the branches, he stopped, looked up, and saw him. He knew who this man was. Jesus called out:

"Hurry and come down out of that tree, Zacchaeus. I am coming to stay at your house today!"

Surprised but happy, Zacchaeus scrambled down the tree and led Jesus to his house. The other people also were surprised, but not so happy. They muttered to themselves, as many people had done before. They said,

"He's gone to be the guest of that miserable, cheating traitor of a taxgatherer!"

But Zacchaeus became a changed man that day. He said to Jesus:

"I am going to give half my money to the poor. And if I have cheated anybody I shall give back four times as much as I took."

Then Jesus was glad that he had called Zacchaeus down from the tree.

"You have been saved from your sins today, Zacchaeus," he said.

Jesus was glad that he had found at least one rich man who did not love his money more than he loved God. Zacchaeus had not been a good man. He was not like the rich young man who had kept all God's commandments since he was a boy. But when he heard Jesus speak to him, he knew that he had been in the wrong. He was ready to do what he could to show that he knew how he had sinned.

"This is what I came for," Jesus said, "to look for sinners like this man and to save them."

When Jesus got to Jerusalem, it was going to cost him a great deal to help men find a new life. But whatever it might cost him, it would be worth the price.

11. Nearing the City

PASSOVER TIME had almost come, so Jesus had to be on his way. Jericho was left behind, and Jesus and the disciples pushed across the hills and desert land that lay east of Jerusalem.

This was the country Jesus had crossed the first time he went to the Passover feast. That was twenty years ago, when he was a boy of twelve, and Joseph and Mary had taken him to the feast in the great city. The stones were just as hard now as they had been then. The land was as dreary to see as it had ever been, and the desert as dry. And yet there were just as many pilgrims from all parts of Palestine traveling

up to Jerusalem, going, as their fathers did before them, to keep the Passover in the holy city of the Jews. In a little while a shout would go up, and many a party would burst into song. They would sing:

"'I was glad when they said unto me,
Let us go into the house of the Lord. . . .
Pray for the peace of Jerusalem:
They shall prosper that love thee.'"

A few days more, and they would sacrifice their lambs in the Temple. They would pray God to be good to the Jews, and to save them from their enemies. A few nights more, and they would sit down to eat the roasted flesh of the lambs at the Passover feast; and when they had eaten they would sing:

"'O give thanks unto the Lord, for he is good:
For his mercy endureth for ever.'"

Jesus and the disciples came out of the desert, and paused among the olive groves near the village of Bethany. Now only the Mount of Olives and the brook called Kidron stood between Jesus and Jerusalem. Already the Passover pilgrims were pouring through the gates of the city and up to the Temple. It was hard for all the pilgrims to find places to stay during the week of the Passover. Here at Bethany, Jesus had friends who loved him, and here he found a place in which to stay.

A man named Simon, whom Jesus once cured of the dreaded leprosy, had a house in Bethany where Jesus was welcome. There also was a woman in Bethany whose name was Mary. She thought that nothing was too much to give to Jesus. Like another woman who once made the Pharisees angry, she came to Jesus when he sat at dinner in Simon's house and poured precious ointment on his head.

But this time it was not the Pharisees who were angry, for there were no Pharisees in the house. It was Jesus' own disciples, especially Judas Iscariot, who said that it was wrong to waste anything that cost as much as the ointment. Judas spoke up and said, "Why was not this ointment sold, and the money given to the poor?"

Judas did not really care about the poor. He looked after the money for Jesus and the disciples, and when he wanted any, he secretly helped himself out of what belonged to all of them. He thought that if the precious ointment had been sold, there would have been more money in the purse he carried.

When Jesus heard the disciples complaining about Mary's gift, he said: "Let her alone. This is a good thing that she has done. There will always be poor people, and you can give them all you like after I am gone. But you will not have *me* always. You know your custom is that when your loved ones die you put ointment on their bodies before you bury them. Well, Mary has come to get me ready to be buried, before I am even dead. I tell you, this woman's name will be remembered all over the world because of what she did for me today!"

The disciples begrudged Jesus the ointment that a loving woman poured upon his head! That was a bad sign. Many times in these last few months Jesus had had to speak sharply to his disciples. The longer they were with him, the less they seemed to understand the things that he had taught them. Jesus was growing lonelier every day, and the hardest task was still ahead.

One time, when they were on the road, John came to Jesus, feeling very proud of himself.

"Master," he said, "we saw a man curing people who were out of their minds and he was using your name to do it! Naturally we told him he would have to stop. He didn't have any right to use your name, when he wasn't one of us!"

Jesus answered: "You shouldn't have stopped him.

143

If he wasn't doing us any harm, then he was on our side!"

Then there was a terrible scene one day, when Jesus found the disciples quarreling about which of them would be the most important when Jesus became king. Each thought that he ought to have a higher position than the rest.

"You aren't supposed to be looking out for yourselves," Jesus told them. "That's what the Romans do. They want to be kings, and order other people about. But the greatest one of you will be the one who does the most to help others, no matter what it costs him. Which would you rather do—sit down to a dinner and have your food brought to you, or bring the food for somebody else? You'd rather sit down and let a servant wait on you, of course. But I am content to be a servant among you, the servant of everyone."

The disciples could not get over thinking that some people were more important than others, and that they themselves counted for more than anyone else. Once some mothers brought their little children to Jesus, hoping that he would put his hands on them and bless them. The disciples did not think that the children counted for anything, and they were going to send them away. They told the mothers that they ought not to come where they were not wanted.

But Jesus called the little children to him, and said: "Let the little children come to me, and don't stand in their way. God's Kingdom is made up of people like these children. God hasn't any place for a person who thinks himself important. These children aren't pushing themselves forward. They are humble, and it would be better if you were more like them!"

With these words Jesus laid his hands upon the children and gave them his blessing, as the mothers wanted him to do.

Another thing that Jesus said, which the disciples could not understand, was that they ought to forgive anyone who did them an injury. One day Peter came to him and asked: "Lord, if somebody keeps on doing wrong to me, how many times should I forgive him? Seven times, perhaps?"

Peter thought that seven times would be doing very well. But Jesus answered: "*Seven* times! Multiply that by seventy! Forgive him until you have lost count of the times!"

When the disciples heard that, they knew that Jesus meant they should never stop forgiving anyone who wronged them. This seemed to them to be more than they could do unless God helped them. They would need more faith in God. So they said, "Lord, give us more faith than we have."

Then Jesus had to tell them that they really did not have any faith at all. He said: "If your faith were only as big as a mustard seed—the smallest seed there is—you could say to that tree over there, 'Be pulled up and be planted in the sea,' and it would be done."

145

No, the disciples did not have much faith. They did not understand Jesus. They were jealous of one another. They thought that Jesus ought to be a king, and each of them thought that he ought to be the king's right-hand man. The disciples were afraid. If Jesus went up to Jerusalem, they could not tell what would happen. Sometimes they thought it would be best if Jesus would stay out of sight where his enemies could not find him.

Worst of all, there was one of the disciples who was not loyal—Judas Iscariot. Judas was planning something so terrible that no one except Jesus knew what it was.

Jesus could not wait until his disciples understood. He could not wait until they were brave enough, or strong enough or good enough. If he did, he would wait forever. And there was very little time.

There was something that he had to do now—the thing he had planned to do all along. Back in the days when he was all alone in the wilderness, after John baptized him in the Jordan, he knew that this was what he would have to do someday. Now the time had come. He must go back to the Temple, where he had stood and watched the Passover lambs being killed when he was a boy of twelve. He must go and get ready for the Passover.

Jerusalem was about two miles away. He could not stay on in Bethany. He must go to Jerusalem at once.

He called two of his disciples and gave his orders.

"Go into the village, and there you will find a young donkey tied. No one has ever ridden it. Untie it and bring it here. If the owner questions you, tell him, 'The Lord needs this donkey.' He will let you have it at once."

The disciples went to do as they were told, and they did not need to be told twice. They knew what Jesus meant, for they knew the Scriptures. If this was the way Jesus was going to Jerusalem, there was nothing to be afraid of!

For it said in the Scriptures that the Messiah would come into Jerusalem riding upon a donkey. How did the words go?

"Rejoice greatly, O daughter of Zion; shout, O daughter of Jerusalem: behold, thy King cometh unto thee: he is just, and having salvation; lowly, and riding upon an ass, and upon a colt the foal of an ass."

Jesus was going to do it! He was going to ride into Jerusalem as the Messiah! Everyone would know who he was at last, for it said in the Scriptures that this was how the Messiah would come to the city! Let the Jews get ready to receive the King they had waited for so long!

They would have to wait no longer. Messiah—King Messiah—was marching toward his throne.

147

12. In Jerusalem

THE DISCIPLES went to the village, as Jesus told them, and there they found the donkey. They untied it, and led it away. Some of them put their clothes on the donkey's back, for a king must ride in comfort. Others spread their clothes out on the street, for a king should ride in state.

Jesus got on the donkey, and started for Jerusalem. The disciples walked ahead. When they had almost reached the city, the disciples began to shout. Jesus used to say that they must not tell anyone that he was the Messiah. But now they could tell the whole world, for Jesus wanted everyone to know. They were glad that they did not have to be quiet any longer.

They shouted, "Hosanna!" It meant, "Save us," and was a cry of welcome. They shouted the words of a psalm: "'Hosanna to the son of David: Blessed is he that cometh in the name of the Lord; Hosanna in the highest.'"

The city was crowded with travelers from all over Palestine, and from foreign countries too. They were the pilgrims who had come for the Passover feast.

The crowds saw the procession coming. They saw the donkey, and they remembered what the Scriptures said. They remembered that that was how the Messiah would come riding in. They heard the shouting, and they understood the words. They knew that that was what people would sing when the Messiah came.

Some of the crowds began to shout with the disciples. A great cry of "Hosanna!" went ringing down the street. Everyone seemed to be saying it. "Blessed is he that cometh in the name of the Lord." Some cut branches from the trees, and waved them before the Messiah. It was a royal welcome.

Only the priests and the rulers and the Pharisees were sorry to see Jesus come.

"What is there we can do?" they said to one another. "Look, the whole world has gone after him!"

The excitement spread through the city. There were strangers there who had never heard of Jesus.

"Who is this?" they asked.

Others who knew him answered, "Why, this is Jesus, the prophet from Nazareth in Galilee."

Jesus went into the Temple and looked about at the crowds which thronged it. This was his Father's house and his house. These were his Father's people and his people.

The king for whom the Jews had been waiting had come at last to reign.

In the evening, Jesus and the disciples returned to Bethany to sleep.

The next day Jesus returned to Jerusalem and again went to the Temple. This time he carried a whip.

In the Court of the Gentiles the money was clinking as it had done when Jesus was a boy. At tables sat the men who grew rich by exchanging the money of visitors for coins used in Jerusalem. Others were selling doves for sacrifice. The poor had to pay heavily to worship God in his own house.

Jesus strode down the room with the whip in his hand, and upset the tables where the money was. When the men jumped up from their chairs, he drove them out of the Temple. Then he drove the sheep and the cattle out after the men.

"It is written in the Scriptures: God's house shall be a house of prayer. But you have made it into a den of thieves and robbers!" he cried.

This was too much for the priests of the temple, and all the important men who ruled Jerusalem. The next day some of the rulers came to Jesus and said:

"What right have you to do these things? Who told you that you could act like this?"

So far, Jesus had never said that he was the Messiah. He had only acted as if he was the Messiah. The rulers hoped that he would say something they could punish him for. But Jesus was too quick for them. He said:

"I'll answer your question if you answer a question of mine. When John the Baptist used to preach to you and baptize people, who gave him the right to do that?"

Then the rulers did not know what to say. They thought to themselves:

Now if we say that John was sent by God to preach, he will say, "Why didn't you listen to him, then?"

If we say that John didn't have any right to preach, the people will be angry and will likely kill us; for everyone still thinks that John the Baptist was a great prophet sent by God himself.

So all they said was, "We don't know—we can't tell."

"Very well," Jesus retorted, "neither am I going to tell you what right I have to do these things!"

Every day that week, Jesus came and taught in the Temple. Several times his enemies tried to trick him into saying something that would turn the people against him, but Jesus always had an answer which silenced them. Once they came and asked, "Should we pay taxes to the Romans?"

That was a hard question. All the Jews hated the Romans, and if Jesus said that it was their duty to pay the taxes, everybody would hate him too. But if he said they should not pay the taxes—well, they could count on the Roman governor to settle with Jesus then.

"Show me a penny," Jesus replied.

Someone handed him a piece of Roman money. There was a man's picture stamped on one side of it. Jesus said, "Whose picture is that?"

"Why," they answered, "that is a picture of Caesar, the emperor of Rome."

"All right," said Jesus, "do whatever your duty is to Caesar and his government. You will have to decide about that for yourselves. And also do your duty to God!"

It was such a clever answer that no one had a word to say. And Jesus still had not said anything that he could be punished for.

But he said a great deal to make his enemies angry. About the Pharisees he spoke the hardest words he ever said.

"Watch out for the scribes and the Pharisees," he told the people, "and don't be like them. They love to walk around in their long white robes, and to have everybody bow to them in the street, and to sit in the best seats in the synagogues and at dinners. All the time they are taking money from poor widows and they try to cover it up by making long prayers."

Turning to the Pharisees themselves, he went on: "Woe to you Pharisees! You are like graves with rotting bodies in them, which people walk over without knowing what is underneath. Nobody knows how bad you are. You snakes! How can you escape the punishment which God is bringing upon you?"

He left the Pharisees and went into the Temple,

where people were making their gifts to God. Many rich men came in, and put large sums of money in the money box. Then came a poor widow who put two small coins into the box.

Jesus called his disciples to him, and said:

"I tell you, this poor widow has given more than all these rich people are giving. For the rich have plenty of money, and it doesn't cost them anything to give what they do. But this poor woman needs her money, and she has given all she has."

With many words and stories he taught the people who thronged around him on the days of that week. And this was the last story he ever told:

"Someday I shall sit upon my throne, and judge all the nations of the earth. To some people I will say:

"'Come—my Heavenly Father loves you. Take the reward he has planned for you to have. For I was hungry, and you gave me food. I was thirsty, and you gave me something to drink. I was a stranger, and you took me into your homes. I had nothing to wear, and you gave me clothes. I was sick, and in prison, and you came to visit me!'

"Then these people will be surprised, and say, 'Lord. when did we ever do anything for you?'

"And I will say: 'You were kind to the poor and the sick and the hungry, who did not count for anything on earth. You did not know it at the time, but when you did a kindness to them, it was to me you really did it.'

"Then I will say to others: 'Go away. God wants nothing to do with you! For I was hungry, and thirsty, and naked, and sick, and in prison, and you did nothing at all for me.'

"These people will also be surprised. They will say: 'Lord, when did we ever see you hungry, or thirsty, or naked, or sick, or in prison? If we had seen you needing anything, we would have helped you!'

"And I will say: 'Many poor people needed your help, and you did not help them. When you failed them, you failed me. And now it is too late!'"

The priests and the rulers did not know what to do about Jesus. *The Messiah, indeed!* they thought. They hated him, and they were afraid of him. They were afraid of the Romans too. What would the Roman governor say if he heard that there was someone in Jerusalem pretending to be King of the Jews?

The priests and the rulers wanted to kill Jesus. That was all they talked about. But they did not know how it was to be done. For whenever Jesus came to Jerusalem, great crowds gathered around him. None of the priests dared to lay a finger on him in the open. The crowds would never let them. It seemed to the people as if the Messiah might have come at last.

But something had to be done, the priests and the rulers said. The week was going by. The Feast of the Passover was nearly there.

157

"We shall have to do away with Jesus quietly," someone said.

"Yes," the others agreed, "we can't wait till the day of the Passover. If we should do anything to him on that day, there would be a riot."

They were at their wits' end to know how to get rid of Jesus. The craftiest men in Jerusalem could not think what to do.

There was a knock at the door. It was one of Jesus' twelve disciples, who had come to see the priests and rulers.

His name? His name was Judas Iscariot.

"What will you give me," Judas said, "if I turn Jesus over to you?"

The priests and rulers could hardly believe their ears.

"Thirty pieces of silver you shall have," they cried, "if you give us Jesus!"

So for thirty pieces of silver Judas agreed to show them where Jesus was, at some time when there was no one around but the twelve disciples.

"Send soldiers when I tell you," Judas said. "The other disciples will all be there, and the soldiers won't know which man to take. But I will go up to Jesus and kiss him. The man I kiss will be the one you want."

Some dark night soon, a quiet place with no one around to see—and nobody would have to worry about Jesus of Nazareth any more!

13. The Last Night

It was Thursday. On Friday afternoon the lambs would be killed for the Passover, and on Friday evening all good Jews would sit down to eat the lambs at the Passover feast. The disciples wondered where Jesus was planning to celebrate the feast with them.

But Jesus did not wait until Friday to have a meal with all his disciples. On Thursday he sent two of them into Jerusalem from Bethany. He told them the name of the man to whom they were to go.

"Go to this man," said Jesus, "and tell him that I said the time has come. He will show you where we are going to have supper tonight. Then you can get the supper ready."

That evening Jesus and the twelve disciples met together at the house in Jerusalem. On the second floor there was a room, where food was spread upon the table.

As they were eating supper, Jesus suddenly spoke. "One of you is a traitor!"

Everyone stopped eating. And each one of the twelve disciples thought of his own sins. Each one

wondered if he were loyal enough to Jesus. Each one cried out:

"Master, is it I?"

Jesus only answered:

"It is one of you twelve men, eating with me now. It would have been better for that traitor if he had never been born!"

A moment later Judas Iscariot slipped quietly out of the door. The other disciples did not know where he had gone.

Jesus spoke again: "I wanted so much to eat the Passover feast with you this year, before I suffer. But I shall not eat it again with you until a better day, when we shall all be together once more."

He took up a piece of bread, and said a prayer of thanks to God. Then he broke the bread, and passed the pieces among the disciples—only eleven of them now. He said words that they did not understand.

"Take and eat this. This is my body."

He took a cup of wine, and once more he gave thanks. Then he passed the cup among the disciples, saying:

"Drink—all of you—drink of this wine. It is my blood, which I am going to shed so that the sins of many people may be forgiven. And in the days to come, do this same thing often, always remembering me."

Then they sang a hymn together and walked out into the night air and went up the Mount of Olives.

As they walked, Jesus said to the disciples:

"You will all desert me tonight. For it is written in the Scriptures that when something happens to the shepherd the sheep will go away in all directions. However, I shall meet you again."

Peter spoke up, and said bravely,

"Even if everyone else deserts you, I will not!"

Jesus answered: "Before the rooster crows at sunrise to tell you that morning has come, you will have said three times that you do not even know me."

But Peter cried out that even if he died for it he would be true to Jesus. And all the other disciples said the same.

Presently they came to a grove called Gethsemane. It was late. Jesus said to the disciples,

"Sit here, while I go and pray."

He took only Peter and James and John with him,

and went a little way apart from the rest. To the three disciples he said:

"I am greatly troubled. I do not know how I can bear it any longer. Wait here, and stay awake with me."

Going a few steps farther on, Jesus fell on his knees and began to pray aloud:

"O my Father, if it is possible, take this cup away; do not let these things happen to me! Yet not my will, but thine, be done."

When he had prayed this way, he came back to Peter and James and John. All three were fast asleep. Jesus woke Peter up, and said:

"What! Couldn't you stay with me for one short hour? Stay awake and pray. Pray for yourselves. You are going to need strength. You are not so strong as you want to be."

He left them again, and once more he fell on his knees and prayed,

"O my Father, if I must suffer these things, thy will be done."

When he returned, the disciples again were sleeping. They were too tired to stay awake.

A third time he went apart from them and prayed. He prayed in the same words he had used before. And suddenly he began to feel stronger. He rose from his knees at last, and came back to the disciples. His voice broke in upon their sleep:

"Are you still sleeping? Well, you've slept long

enough! My time is up. I am going to be turned over to sinners now! Get up! Look, the traitor is coming!"

While he was still speaking, a crowd of soldiers carrying swords and clubs burst into the grove. Judas Iscariot was leading them. Judas ran to Jesus and kissed him, saying,

"Hail, Master!"

Jesus answered, "Well, friend—what have you come to do?"

Then a band of men laid their hands on Jesus, and held him so that he could not escape.

Peter was wide-awake by now. He had brought a sword with him. Pulling it out, he cut off the ear of a man in the crowd.

Jesus said to Peter: "Put your sword away. My Father gave me these things to suffer. He would save me now if I asked him. But that is not the way it is to be."

Then Jesus turned to the crowd of soldiers, and said:

"Have you come to arrest me with swords and clubs, as though I were a robber? Every day I was in the Temple teaching, and you could have taken me then, but you never laid a hand on me. But this is what the Scriptures said would happen to the Messiah."

The disciples could stand no more. They left Jesus standing there, and in terror they fled away.

14. The Last Day

THE SOLDIERS bound Jesus and led him back to Jerusalem. They took him to the palace of the high priest. All the chief priests and rulers were gathered there in a council meeting.

The council had already decided that Jesus would have to die, but it was hard to find a reason for killing him. They had to prove that Jesus had said or done something for which he could be put to death. They found a great many people who came and told lies about Jesus, but no two of them told the same story.

At last the high priest, whose name was Caiaphas, stood up and said to Jesus:

"You hear all the things that are being said about you. Aren't you going to defend yourself?"

Jesus did not say a word.

The high priest spoke again:

"In the name of the living God I ask you: Are you the Christ—the Messiah—the Son of God?"

Jesus answered:

"You have said it."

That was all the council wanted to hear. Caiaphas tore his own clothes in anger, and shouted:

"Why do we need any more witnesses? You have heard him say it with his own mouth. He says he's God! What do you think about it?"

And the whole council answered,

"He ought to be put to death."

Then some of them spat in his face. They covered his eyes, and slapped him, and shouted:

"If you were the Messiah, you would know who hit you! Tell us, you Messiah you—tell us who hit you!"

Meanwhile, in another room of the palace, there stood a disciple who was losing whatever faith he had once had. It was Peter. One of the other disciples, who knew the high priest, had gone ahead, and he had told the maid to let Peter in.

The maid looked at Peter and said, "You were with Jesus, weren't you?"

"I don't know what you're talking about," said Peter.

The night was cool, and the servants of the high priest were standing around a fire they had made to keep themselves warm. Peter went over and began to warm himself too. Somebody else said to him,

"You are one of Jesus' disciples."

Peter's faith was all gone.

"Man," he said, "I certainly am not!"

But after a while another person spoke up and said:

"Of course you are one of Jesus' disciples. You are from Galilee. We can tell from the way you talk."

Peter began to curse and swear, saying, "I don't even know this Jesus that you are talking about!"

At that moment the rooster began to crow. At the same time Jesus passed by the doorway, and looked at Peter.

Peter remembered what Jesus had said, "Before the rooster crows, you will three times say that you do not know me."

Peter went out of the palace, and wept bitterly.

The great council of the Jews might say that a man deserved to die, but they could not put anyone to death. Only the Roman governor could do that.

The Roman governor, whose name was Pontius Pilate, was in Jerusalem for the Passover. As soon as it was daylight, the council took Jesus over to Pilate's palace.

When Judas Iscariot saw what was happening, he suddenly realized what he had done. He came to the chief priests, and brought them back the thirty pieces of silver they had given him for turning traitor. He cried out:

"I have sinned! I betrayed a man who never did any wrong!"

The chief priests shrugged their shoulders.

"That's nothing to us," they said. "Take your money and go!"

But Judas threw the money down on the floor and ran out. He took a rope, and found a tree, and hanged himself, for, after betraying Jesus, he could not bear to live.

Meanwhile Jesus was standing before Pilate. The council had told Pilate that Jesus was claiming to be the King of the Jews. They said that he was stirring up the whole country against Caesar. They thought that Pilate would put him to death for that, because the Romans would be afraid that Jesus would lead a revolt against the Roman government.

Pilate said to Jesus,

"Well, are you the King of the Jews?"

Jesus answered simply,

"You have said it."

Then the priests and rulers burst out with all kinds of evil stories about Jesus.

Pilate spoke to Jesus again, and said:

"Aren't you going to say anything? Listen to what they are saying about you!"

But Jesus did not speak. Pilate was astonished. He could see that the only reason the council had brought

Jesus to him was that they were jealous of Jesus and hated him.

By now a large crowd had gathered to watch the trial. Many of the people in it had been Jesus' followers, but they followed him no longer. When they saw Jesus being tried like a criminal they decided that their priests and rulers had been right all along. They began to talk against Jesus, among themselves.

Pilate wondered how he could let Jesus go. Suddenly he remembered a Jewish custom: every Passover a prisoner was set free.

Pilate said: "Every year at this time I set a prisoner free. Now you can have your choice. You know we have a man named Barabbas in jail—he's the fellow that started a rebellion a little while ago. We were going to crucify him. And now here is Jesus. Which

one shall I let go? Barabbas the murderer or Jesus who is called the Christ?"

A great shout went up,

"Barabbas!"

Pilate did not know what to do now. He spoke again to the crowd,

"Well, what shall I do to Jesus who is called the Christ?"

Again there was a great shout:

"Crucify him! Hang him up on a cross till he is dead!"

Everyone seemed to be against Jesus now. However, Pilate tried once more.

"But," he protested, "I can't find that he has been guilty of any crime!"

The Jewish rulers replied, "We have a law which says he ought to die because he pretends to be the Son of God."

Pilate was worried now. He spoke to Jesus again, and again Jesus did not answer.

"Aren't you going to speak to me?" Pilate asked. "Don't you know that I can crucify you or let you go?"

Jesus answered, "You wouldn't have any power over me unless God had given it to you."

Pilate, when he heard this, tried once more to save Jesus. But the crowd was bigger, and louder, and more bloodthirsty than ever. Everyone was shouting:

"Crucify! Crucify!"

"Shall I crucify your king?" asked Pilate.

The chief priests of the Jews, who hated Caesar, answered,

"We have no king except Caesar!"

Pilate was too weak to hold out any longer. He was beginning to wonder what Caesar would say if he heard that Pilate refused to crucify a man who claimed to be king of the Jews.

"Take him," Pilate said. "Take him, and crucify him."

But before the crucifixion came the scourging. Jesus was bound and beaten with long leather thongs which had cruel pieces of glass and lead fastened to them so that they would hurt all the more. When that was over, and his back was covered with cuts and bruises, the Roman soldiers who had scourged him wanted some more sport. They dressed Jesus in a purple robe. They made a wreath, like the one that the Roman emperor wore—only this one was made of thorns, which stuck into Jesus' head so that the blood ran down his face. Some of the soldiers spat on him; others made fun of him, bowing down and saying,

"Hail, king of the Jews!"

Then the soldiers stripped the purple clothes off Jesus, and put his own clothes back on him, and led him outside the city to be crucified. He was too worn out to carry his own cross, as those who were to be crucified usually did, so the soldiers forced a man of Cyrene named Simon to carry it for him.

When they reached a hill called Calvary, they laid
the cross down on the ground, and stripped Jesus of
his clothes. They put Jesus on the cross, and stretched
out his arms. They drove a nail through each hand,
and one through his feet, fastening him to the cross.
Then they stood the cross upright, and let Jesus hang
there. On the top of it was written: "This is the King
of the Jews." There was a cross on either side of him,
with a thief hanging on each one.

Jesus said, "Father, forgive them; for they know
not what they do."

The soldiers took his clothes, and divided them up
among themselves. His coat was too good to tear up,
so they threw dice to see which one of them would
get it.

Jesus was offered a drink which would have made
the pain easier to bear, but he would not take it.
People passed to and fro in front of the cross, shouting
insults.

"He saved others, but he can't save himself."
One of the thieves turned his head and called out to
him angrily,

"If you are the Christ, save yourself and us too!"
But the other thief spoke out of his pain:

"Don't you fear God, seeing that we are all going
to die? Aren't you afraid to talk that way? We deserve to die; but this man never did anything wrong."

Then, turning to Jesus, he said, "Lord, remember
me when you come to your Kingdom."

Jesus said to him,

"I tell you, today you will be with me in heaven."

Near the cross stood Jesus' mother and other wom-
en who loved him. John the disciple was also there.
Jesus called to his mother and John, and said:

"Mother, from now on John will be your son. John,
this is your mother."

John took Jesus' mother to his own house.

The hours passed by. It was about time for the
Passover lambs to be killed in the city. Clouds were
beginning to cover the sun, and it was growing dark
although it was not yet night.

Jesus cried out,

"My God, my God, why hast thou forsaken me?"

There was a stir of interest in the crowd. *Let's see
what will happen now*, they thought.

Jesus was becoming weaker. He said, "I am thirsty."

A soldier dipped a sponge in vinegar, and held it
up on a stick to Jesus' lips so that he could drink.

Jesus cried out once more:

"It is finished. Father, into thy hands I give my spirit."

His head sank down upon his chest. There was a loud sound like a clap of thunder, and the earth shook.

In the silence that followed, a Roman soldier spoke.

"This man—" he said, "this man was indeed the Son of God."

But Jesus did not hear him. For Jesus was dead.

When evening came, a man named Joseph of Arimathaea went to see Pilate. Joseph was a rich man, and much respected; and he had believed in Jesus. He went secretly to Pilate, for he was afraid of the Jews. He asked Pilate if he might have Jesus' body, and Pilate gave permission.

Joseph came then to the cross, and took down Jesus' body. He wrapped it in a white linen cloth, and had it carried away to a tomb which had been dug out of the rock. Not until after the Sabbath could Jesus' family and friends come to put spices on the body of him whom they loved.

Jesus' body was laid inside the tomb, and a great stone was rolled against the door.

Standing there was a woman named Mary Magdalene with Mary the mother of Jesus. They watched while the body of Jesus, so dear to them, was laid away to rest.

15. The Victorious King

AT SUNRISE the day following the Sabbath, three women came to the garden where Jesus was buried. They came, as the custom was, to put ointments and spices on the body of Jesus.

On the way they remembered that a great stone had been rolled against the door of the tomb. They wondered how they would get in.

"Who will roll the stone away?" they asked each other.

But when they reached the tomb, they found that the stone had been rolled back. Someone had been there before them; the door was open.

The women went through the door of the tomb. A young man in white clothes was sitting on one side. Seeing their amazement, the young man spoke:

"Do not be surprised. You are looking for Jesus of Nazareth, who was crucified. He is not here. He is risen from the dead. Look! There is the place where he was!"

They looked, and they saw that his body was no longer there.

The young man went on, "Go quickly, and tell this to his disciples: 'Jesus is alive.'"

The women ran out of the tomb, trembling with fright and with surprise. One of the women was Mary Magdalene. As she ran, she saw two of the disciples coming, John and Peter. She cried out to them:

"Someone has taken Jesus' body out of the tomb. We don't know where they have put it!"

John and Peter began to run toward the tomb. John ran faster, and got there first. He looked through the door, and there he saw the white cloths that Jesus' body had been wrapped in, but there was no body in them any longer. Peter caught up to John, and ran right into the tomb. He too saw the folded cloths. John and Peter went away to their homes, not knowing what to think.

Meanwhile Mary Magdalene had come back. She stood in the garden near the tomb, weeping as though her heart would break. She turned around, and saw that a man was standing near her. He spoke to her, and said:

"Why are you crying? For whom are you looking?"

Mary thought that the man must be the gardener.

Through her tears she said:

"Sir, if you have carried away the body of my Lord, tell me where you have laid him, and I will go and take him away."

The man said softly,

"Mary!"

She looked again. She knew that voice. It was Jesus—Jesus calling her name!

She cried out,

"Master!"

She moved as though to take hold of him. Jesus spoke again. It was really he.

"Do not try to hold me here. I am going to my Father in heaven. But now go and tell that to the disciples. Tell them that I am going to my Father."

And Mary went and told the disciples,

"I have seen the Lord!"

Afterward, no one could ever remember clearly all that happened on that day. No one knew what to make of it all. No one knew whether to believe that Jesus was really alive.

Late that afternoon, two disciples were walking along the road from Jerusalem to the village of Emmaus. They talked of what had happened on Friday, and now on Sunday. As they were talking, a stranger joined them. The stranger said,

"What is it that you are talking about?"

The disciples stopped. They were almost too

sad to speak any more, but one of them answered,

"Are you the only visitor to Jerusalem who doesn't know the things that have been happening there these last few days?"

"What things?" the stranger asked.

The disciples replied:

"Why, all about Jesus of Nazareth. He was a great prophet and teacher. The chief priests and the rulers had him crucified. We had hoped that he was the Messiah, who was going to save the Jewish people.

But now it is two days since he was put to death, and nothing has happened—though there were some women who went to the tomb and came away saying that he was risen from the dead."

The stranger said:

"O you foolish men—so slow to believe what it says in the Prophets! Don't you see that the Messiah had to suffer this way in order to be King?"

Then he explained everything in the Scriptures about the Messiah. He spoke to them of how the Prophet Isaiah had said long ago:

"He was despised and cast out by men; a man of sorrows and full of grief; and no one would look at him. He was hurt, because we were so sinful. He suffered for our sakes. He was killed like a lamb, and he did not try to defend himself."

The stranger explained that Isaiah was talking about the Messiah. The Messiah was to be humble, and sacrifice himself, like one of the lambs at the Passover feast. Isaiah meant that the only one who could help others was the one who was willing to suffer for others. The Messiah never wanted to be a king like other kings. He did not want to lord it over others. He wanted to love them, and to give his life for them.

"And so," the stranger went on, "you ought not to be sad, thinking that Jesus is not the Messiah after all. Jesus has lived and died as the Scriptures said the Messiah would. His love and his sufferings prove that he really is the Messiah. And if his believers love one another, as he has loved them, and sacrifice themselves as he has done, they will have peace and joy."

As the three walked on, the stranger talked. When they reached Emmaus, they came to the home of one of the disciples. They said to the stranger:

"Come in and stay with us. It is evening. The day is nearly over."

They went into the house. Someone lighted the lamps, and food was placed before them.

The stranger took some bread, and said a prayer of thanks, and broke the bread.

The disciples had seen something like that before— breaking bread. They looked up quickly.

Why! This man was not a stranger at all. It was Jesus. They knew him as they looked into his face. And as they looked, he vanished out of their sight, and they were alone again.

They said to each other,

"Didn't you have a strange feeling, as he talked to us along the road and explained the Scriptures?"

Although it was now night, they returned to Jerusalem at once. They found the other disciples and told their story.

"The Lord is indeed alive!" they said. "We knew him the moment he broke the bread!"

While they were speaking, Jesus was suddenly among them once again. Jesus said,

"Peace be with you."

They were frightened then, but Jesus spoke again. "Do not be afraid," he said. "I am not a spirit."

They still could hardly believe it. It seemed too good to be true. And while they stood there, not daring to believe that Jesus was alive, he said,

"Have you anything here to eat?"

They set a piece of broiled fish before him, and Jesus sat down to supper.

One of the disciples was not there when Jesus appeared to the others. His name was Thomas. And no matter what the others said, Thomas could not believe that Jesus was alive again.

"Unless," he said, "I see in his hands the marks that the nails made when they crucified him, and unless I put my finger into those marks, I will not believe."

Eight days later the disciples were all together. This time Thomas was with the others. The doors were shut.

Suddenly Jesus appeared again, and said as he had said before,

"Peace be with you."

Then Jesus turned to Thomas, and said,

"Put your finger into the nail holes in my hand, and doubt no more, but believe in me!"

Thomas fell down on his knees. He cried out, "My Lord and my God!"

Jesus said to him:

"You believe in me because you have seen me with your own eyes. It is still better when people believe even though they have not seen me."

After this the disciples saw Jesus many times and at many places. But a day came at last after which they did not see him on earth again.

On this day Jesus appeared to them outside Jerusalem, and said:

"All power has been given to me in heaven and earth. I am Lord and King of all men. Go and tell people of every nation about me, so that they will believe in me. Baptize everybody in my name. Teach them everything that I have taught you. You will not be alone, for although you do not see me, I shall be with you always."

Then Jesus said to them: "Wait a little while. Wait in Jerusalem, and someday soon you will know that the time has come to go out and preach. God will give you the power to make other people believe in me as their Saviour. You shall tell about me in Jerusalem, and in the country all around; in Samaria, and in the farthest parts of the earth."

He lifted up his hands, and blessed them. And as he blessed them, a cloud covered him, and they did not see him any more.

Jesus had gone home to his Father.

They stared up into the sky, where he seemed to have gone. As they looked, they heard voices saying:

"You men of Galilee, why do you stand looking up into the sky? The Lord Jesus will come again!"

Then they remembered that they had work to do before they again would see Jesus. They had to go and preach, as Jesus had told them. They had to tell about him to all people everywhere.

187

They walked back into Jerusalem. They had to wait; but now they were not waiting for Christ the Saviour to come. They were waiting only for the sign that would tell them it was time to go out and preach that Christ had already come.

The Passover was finished for another year, and the farmers of Palestine had work to do. The warm spring weather spread over the land, and the wheat was growing in the fields and on the hillsides. Farmers reaped their crops, and gathered in the grain, and got ready for another feast at Jerusalem. For when the wheat was gathered, it was time to go and give thanks to God for the harvest, at the Feast of Pentecost.

The disciples waited while the weeks of spring went by. Every day they went to the Temple and praised God for his goodness, because they knew that Christ had come.

Seven weeks passed by. The hot sun ripened the crops, and the farmers cut their grain. The Day of Pentecost came around, and the streets of Jerusalem were thronged again. There were men there from near and far, from every country of which anyone had ever heard. The harvest was over, and the feast was on!

That morning the disciples were all together when they heard the sound. It was a sound like the rushing wind, bringing messages from God. They saw a vision too, and what they saw seemed like tongues of fire, coming down to each one of them so that all could speak what God wanted them to say.

The disciples went out and began to speak. Everyone who heard them understood what they were saying.

Excitement went through the city.

"This is strange!" the people said. "We have come from near and far. We speak many different languages. Yet when these men tell us about the wonderful things that God has done, we understand what they are telling us. What is it that has happened?"

Peter stood up beside the other disciples, and boldly raised his voice:

"Listen to me, everyone who is here at Jerusalem! You have read in the Scriptures how God said that he would send his Holy Spirit to his people. That is what has happened! The time has come to preach to you! Therefore, listen to my words.

"God sent Jesus of Nazareth to you, and he did many wonderful things among you, which you saw for yourselves. God let you take him and put him to death with your own wicked hands. But it was not possible for him to be held forever by death. God has raised him up from the dead, and we have seen it! He is King; and he has given us the power to tell you about him, and you can hear what we are telling you. Let everybody know this for a fact: this very Jesus whom you crucified is Lord and Christ!"

And when the people heard these words, they were greatly troubled.

"What shall we do?" they cried.

Peter answered:

"Repent! Give up your sins, and begin a new life! Believe in Jesus Christ, and let us baptize you in his name. Then your sins will be forgiven, and he will send his Holy Spirit to change you!"

Many were glad when they heard this, and they were baptized in Jesus' name. That very day about three thousand people became believers and followers of Christ. They joined with those who had been disciples before, praying together, and sharing with each other everything they had. Jesus had a Church, which believed that he was Christ the Saviour.

Every day many more were added to the Church. Every day the Church of Jesus Christ grew stronger.

It grew like the grainfields in the spring.

SCRIPTURE REFERENCES